MOON CHASE

Across the bleak and tortured surface of the moon they fled—the visionary scientist, Mark Randall, and his brilliant, beautiful companion, Ann Willett.

Close behind were their pursuers, the crack agents of the BPS, security arm of the vast, all-powerful tyranny that ruled over Earth.

Only the two fugitives could block the total enslavement of all mankind. But time was running out, the deadly laser guns were homing in—and all that remained for them was one last desperate gamble. . . .

Whisper from the Stars

JEFF SUTTON

A DELL BOOK

Published by
DELL PUBLISHING CO., INC.
750 Third Avenue, New York, New York 10017

Dell ® TM 681510, Dell Publishing Co., Inc.
Printed in the United States of America
First printing—February 1970

ONE

Nights are the worst.

Those cloudless nights when the moon is gone and the stars gleam down, brittle and harsh—a thousand mocking eyes. Not that they really mock me; that is in my mind. Yet it is mockery of a sort, for I know they hold secrets all but unimaginable to the human mind.

The human mind of this reality, that is.

If that sounds strange it is because, for a brief time, I was allowed to glimpse those secrets, in part at least. I know that *eternity* and *infinity* are but relative concepts, subject to the point of view. I know that man, in some form other than my own, quietly has taken over the universe.

I know because I've lived and died and lived again.

I have seen through time.

I have *seen,* but could a Neanderthaler have understood the complexity of the modern computer had it been explained to him? Could he have understood its purpose? No. He would have stood at the mouth of his cave, his eyes puzzled, much as mine are when I gaze into that blazing, endless firmament. To know and not to know: that is the damnable thing that haunts me.

Days are better.

By day I pursue my work. I make my contacts, get my interviews, write my stories, and send them by radiophone to the *Solar Press.* The better ones I tape for *World Triscreen*, a corporation affiliate.

Because I'm a staff man free to wander, I file stories from all parts of the Earth, and occasionally from the moon and Mars. I've even dispatched stories from the bleak Jovian colonies of Ganymede and Callisto, and once from Titan, that lonely plodder around the great, ringed Saturn. Titan, as you know, is the fartherest outpost of human penetration.

Or was before Mark Randall.

But you know my work. My by-line, *by Joel Blake*, appears in nearly three hundred newspapers, not to mention the score of newsletters which are transmitted to the moon and Mars, and to the OutSat worlds beyond. You must have seen my face on the triscreen a thousand times.

My days are busy; but at nights—those cloudless, moonless nights when I'm alone—I *feel* the stars. Like magnets, they draw me. At such times, often against my will, I'm compelled to go outside, look up into the harsh grate of the sky, gaze at its multi-thousand winking eyes. Gaze and think and listen—wait for a *whisper*.

Worse is when the whisper comes.

It comes from beyond the blaze of lights, from beyond the gulfs of darkness which separate the burning suns. It comes, perhaps, from a thousand or a million or a billion years in the future. Cloaked in infinity and eternity it comes, as I've learned to think of it, as *silent sound*.

"We are here, Joel," the ghostly voice in my mind says. Then I tremble, for I know it is the voice of Mark Randall. Could my eyes penetrate those fearful gulfs, I know I would see him again. I also know Ann Willett would be at his side.

It is then that I feel the awful desolation, know the utter solitude of riding this frail craft of Earth through immensities too great to comprehend. My own sense of insignificance bears down on me.

My time is now: A.D. 2231. Two planets and four moons have been peopled. Disease has been conquered; poverty has been all but banished; war has been thrust into the past. Yet I stand in the primitive dawn of man. I know that now.

I am Neanderthaler, staring upward at the stars. Elsewhere it is high noon; and somewhere else it is dusk. I am speaking of the high noon of human existence, the dusk when all things end. When the universe dies.

That is what the stars tell me.

At such times I flee back to my room, busy myself with work, pour a drink, call a friend—anything to banish the poignant memories. But neither work nor drink nor a casual date holds them back. In the end, lying in bed, I stare upward at the dark ceiling to watch Mark Randall and Ann Willett stride hand-in-hand across the plaster, while the memories dance like moonbeams in my mind.

Ann's eyes, once filled with wistful longing, are smiling; Mark has a laugh on his lips. Then, until sleep mercifully closes my eyes, I relive the way it had been.

It had all started nearly six years before.

TWO

I first met Ann Willett on the patio at Ted Carlson's house. I'd stepped outside, drink in hand, to escape the harsh music of the band Carlson's wife had hired to celebrate some event or other—I forget what, for the parties were endless in those days. I saw her standing alone, unbelievably lovely in the pale moonlight.

My first impression was of honey-colored hair, unswept in the fashion of the day, a tall, graceful body, the profile of a sensitive face sculpted to perfection. Instinctively I knew her eyes would be green; no other color would match such a face. Her head tilted upward; she was watching the stars in silent contemplation. As if aware of my scrutiny, she turned.

"Sorry if I'm intruding," I apologized. I moved closer.

"Not at all," she murmured. She glanced at the sky again. "It's so quiet outside, so peaceful."

"I don't believe we've met." I'm usually quite adroit with words, yet somehow my speech came haltingly. "I'm Joel Blake."

"I know," she acknowledged. "I'm Ann Willett."

"What do you do, aside from escaping noisy house parties to watch the stars?"

"Read, swim, play the violin."

"Violin?" I don't know why I questioned it, as I realized instantly the instrument would fit her to perfection. It was the kind of thing a trained journalist would sense.

"A hobby," she explained.

"I should like to hear you."

She shook her head. "I seldom play for company. It's a mood instrument; that's how I think of it."

"Melancholy?"

"I don't attach words. It's just a feeling."

"Words define feelings," I rebutted.

"Perhaps to a journalist," she acceded. "But it's more than just a feeling. I used the word lightly."

"The next level upward from emotion is thought."

"Yes, it makes me think."

"Which brings us back into a definable realm." I felt pleased with myself. "I can understand how an emotion might seem indefinable, but not a cerebral concept. Words are the vehicles of thought and, by extension, of logic. Nor can logic exist without them."

"I don't believe that's true, Mr. Blake."

"Joel," I corrected.

"Joel." She gave the name a musical ring.

"What do you believe?"

"That what we call logic is a creature of our limitations."

"I don't follow that," I admitted.

"I believe that our senses, and therefore the cortex which feeds on them, are restricted—that we live in a closed loop from which there is no escape. We go around and around like squirrels in a cage, yet somehow can't generate the momentum to break from our own particular orbit. I'm afraid that our logic is what we deduce from a quite restricted environment."

I gazed at her with new respect. I hadn't contemplated such depths from a lovely woman so casually met at a rather noisy house party. "Our orbit is rather large," I suggested.

A smile touched her lips. "It is pitifully small."

"How does all that tie in with the violin?" I asked quietly.

"Have you ever listened to a violin? Really listened? Its voice is the loneliest in the universe. It whispers of things beyond"—she hesitated before adding—"the logic we draw with words."

"It stirs the imagination, yes."

"It's more than that, but perhaps we don't all hear the same things."

"We hear what we expect to hear," I observed.

"Of course." Her eyes mocked me. "We create our worlds from what we know, or believe we know. That's why I said we live in a closed and predictable loop. Our prison is fashioned by our self-imposed limitations."

"Self-imposed?"

"It's not nature that restricts us. It's ourselves."

"And if we break from our orbit?"

"I don't know the answer."

"What kind of a breakthrough do you contemplate?"

"I'm not certain."

"Yet you wonder," I observed.

"That is the greatest gift nature gave us," she said. "Where would we be without the ability to wonder?"

"We'd muddle through; we always have."

"Not without wonder."

I contemplated my empty glass and laughed. "That calls for a drink."

"No, thank you."

"A Martini," I said firmly, "is the best mood-breaker in the world."

"I have no mood to break," she answered quietly. Her expression was unreadable. Despite her protest, I hurried inside, threaded my way across the dance floor, and mixed the drinks myself. Mine was heavy on the Vodka. When I returned outside, Ann Willett had disappeared.

I stared blankly at the empty patio. Perhaps she'd gone inside. The hope was dashed as a car engine purred to life in the driveway. By the time I reached that side of the house, I was too late. Red taillight eyes cut an arc in the darkness as a vehicle swung from the drive, its bubble-top gleaming briefly in the glare of a street lamp before it was lost to view.

"There goes a wonderful evening," I chided myself. It wasn't just that Ann Willett was lovely; it went far beyond that. A girl who listened to the lonely cry of a violin, who heard in it something indefinable to the senses, and related that to man as living in a closed loop from which there was no escape—that *was* unusual.

"Around and around like squirrels in a cage"—her words came back. For a moment I could all but glimpse what she'd meant. In a sense it was true; society was a system of wheels, all spinning madly, none getting anywhere. Or had she a deeper meaning?

I returned inside and sought out Ted Carlson. He was easy to find. He was a slender, pale-faced man who was all the rage since the successful production of his latest play, *Three Steps from Heaven*, and was, at the moment, the center of a coterie of gushing females. It was a situation he enjoyed. The faces of his admirers were far from cordial when I plucked his sleeve and drew him to one side.

"Who's Ann Willett?" I asked.

"Ah, you've met her." His eyes glinted.

"Yeah, but she didn't bother to wait around."

Carlson smirked. "You must have been great company."

"Come off it!" I suppressed my irritation. "Who is she?"

"An astrophysicist," he answered. "One of the best."

"Astrophysicist?"

"On the faculty at UCLA."

"Lord," I groaned. Memory of my trite lecture on words as the vehicles of logic made me wince. She must have pegged me as a prime idiot. "She told me she was a violinist!"

"Tops," he affirmed. His curled lips told me he was laughing at me. "What did you do to frighten her away?"

"We'd scarcely met."

"Then you know her as well as anyone, Joel."

"She's a loner?"

"Not particularly, but neither is she a mixer, at least not in this league. What would you expect when you mix genius with peons?" He was laughing again. "I suspect she occasionally pops up at affairs like this in the hope of meeting someone like herself. Apparently she gave up for the night."

"Big help," I said. At that moment a gorgeous brunette in an iridescent silvery sheath that hugged her naked body crept up behind him and covered his eyes with small hands. Her nails were long, polished talons.

"Guess who?" she cooed.

"A bewitching creature named Elaine," answered Carlson. He removed her hands and turned triumphantly. "See, I'm right. Come on, I'll buy you both a drink."

"No thanks." Pleading business, I turned to leave. At the door, I glanced back. The party looked dreary and flat—a room filled with pallid marionettes. For me, the keen edge of excitement had gone with the red taillights that had vanished in the night.

In my work I meet all kinds of women in all kinds of places—from the offices and parties and cocktail lounges of the big metropolitan centers to the lonely domes of the OutSat worlds. Most are predictable: they respond to their immediate surroundings and to their immediate situations. *Squirrels in a cage.* But not Ann Willett. It was that knowledge that kept her in my mind.

She was an astrophysicist, all right. The four-inch tome *The Great of Science* gave her more than her share of space. "M.A., Mathematics; Ph.D., Astrophysics; Research into the distribution of metastable states of atoms . . ." I read to the end, largely a jargon that I failed to understand. Yet, in some inexplicable way, I felt I knew her better.

Efforts to obtain her phone number were fruitless; it was unlisted. I did manage to get her address. After kicking it around for several days, I decided on the bold approach and drove over to see her.

The house was difficult to locate. Set well back from a winding road in the steep hills a few miles from the university, it was cantilevered out over the edge of a precipitous canyon. Although the hills were solid with houses, the narrow spur on which it stood provided splendid isolation. It held a privacy that few homes enjoyed.

I checked the name on the mailbox before looking up at it. Except for a single lighted window in the upper story, the house was dark. The steep drive that led to it, the pitch of the roof against the stars, the air of solitude the spur afforded—everything screamed of loneliness. With it came the knowledge that she wanted it that way.

Caught with the brashness of my intent, I hesitated. My presence would be an intrusion of the worst sort. At best, she'd consider me extremely impolite and presumptuous. And I had been. Yet how else could I meet her?

As I debated my actions, I heard a high singing sound that reminded me of taut wires in a wind. I rolled back the dome roof to listen. It came again, a thin, plaintive wail that reverberated off the canyon walls.

The silence returned, followed almost immediately by a haunting melody that I believed to be the loneliest I'd ever heard. Elements of fantasy and lyric beauty seemingly were fused in a refrain that gradually developed to the exciting pizzicato chords of the violin. Suddenly it ended, returning seconds later with a ghostly musical dance that reached, echoing, into the deep parts of my mind. It cried of things unknown. When I understood, I felt tremulous.

There was nothing wrong with a beautiful girl playing a violin; nothing that I could put into words. It was just a girl in a lonely house in the hills playing an instrument she loved. Yet I knew it was more than that. Somehow it had to do with the strange things she'd told me. Man, the trapped animal, for whom there was no escape—that was the gist of her words, the gist of the haunting melody that came from the lonely house. To whom was the violin speaking? What strange things did it ask in that language that only she seemed to understand? Idiotic? Perhaps, but that's the way I felt—the violin was an insistent voice that mirrored the torment of her soul. Torment, or was it rapport? I couldn't begin to guess.

One thing I did know: to break in on her now would be absolutely unforgivable. If there was any one moment in which she closed out the world, this was it. Finally the haunting strains died away. Moments later the light in the upper window blinked out, leaving the house shrouded in darkness. Notched against the sky, it seemed unutterably lonely.

Three months later, shortly after my return from Africa, I met her again: we all but collided outside the entrance to San Francisco's Sky Restaurant, on the ninety-second floor of the Golden West Building. "Ann Willett," I exclaimed. "What are you doing here?"

She didn't appear overly happy at the encounter. "I came north for a conference."

"Astrophysics?" I asked severely.

She nodded. "I sneaked away for some shopping."

"And lunch with Joel Blake," I said. I saw her hesitate and added, "I'm a lonely stranger in town."

"I can't imagine that." She eyed me archly but allowed me to guide her to a table inside. When we were seated, she inquired, "What brings you to San Francisco?"

"The usual—chasing news, filing reports. Will-o'-the-wisps," I said. As we chatted, her reserve began to melt. Several times, laughing, she was quite radiant. I decided against mentioning my attempts to contact her again. Nothing in her demeanor suggested it would be welcome. Oh, she was pleasant enough, but the barrier was there.

When we rose to go, I was chagrined to realize that I'd learned practically nothing about her. She'd been extremely adept at turning aside questions related to her work and personal life. It left me with the impression of having viewed her in two dimensions, no depth, yet with the suspicion that the depths were enormous.

Outside I glanced ruefully at my watch. "I'm booked on a four o'clock flight to London," I offered. "You?"

"I return south tomorrow."

"I'm stuck with a tour of the Continent," I admitted, "but I'll be back in a few weeks. Supper and a show?" I gazed expectantly at her.

"I seldom plan ahead."

"Don't be a squirrel in a cage," I reprimanded. "Break from orbit."

She laughed. "All right, supper and a show."

"I'll require a number."

She hesitated briefly before giving one. "Call several days in advance," she warned.

"I'll send a wire from Berlin."

"No, seriously."

"Yes, of course." On that note we parted. I watched her swing away, a slender, graceful woman who, even on the crowded street, appeared to walk alone. It was then that I knew our talk had been just words; I'd never reached her. How could I? Could anyone? She struck me as a real loner. Yet I had one satisfying thought: we both inhabited the same closed loop.

I made my rounds—London, Paris, Berlin, Vienna, a few stops in between. In the latter city I caught wind of a story in Moscow, wound up in Irkutsk near the border of Mongolia, then caught an old-fashioned Mach 3 stratojet to Hong Kong. The next evening I was back in Los Angeles.

I called Ann three times before I managed a date for supper and a show. That was a small beginning, but it was a beginning. Still, she would never allow me to pick her up. Invariably, when we had a date, she would meet me in town.

Sporadically, between jaunts around the globe, our dates continued in that vein for more than a year. Our talk usually was chit-chat, seldom personal. When it was serious, it usually involved the larger issues of the day—the dangers associated with moving several of the bigger asteroids into Earth orbit to facilitate their mining, and the logistics problems related to supplying the ever expanding scientific and mining communities on the moon, Mars, the OutSat worlds beyond; things like that. On such occasions it seemed that I did most of the talking, she the listening; yet I was fairly certain she was far better versed than I on many of the subjects.

Yet even those conversations had no real depth. It wasn't so much the subject matter as the feeling I had when we discussed them. She always held herself just beyond my reach. Only once, when speaking of her work, did she exhibit bitterness.

"A person isn't permitted to pursue his own research," she exclaimed. "The government controls every facet of it."

"Well, if you're working under government contract. . . ."

"What isn't under government contract?" she interrupted. Her eyes blazed, the first display of temper I'd seen.

"Can't you still work as an individual?"

"Without lab facilities?" Her tone was brittle. "That's the weapon—the government funds the labs, ties them up. It's almost impossible to pursue individual research."

"But you still get credit for your work."

"Is that important? Besides, it's not true." She shook her head. "Any discovery or breakthrough of any consequence promptly goes into the government hopper, is classified. That prevents any real discussion of it in the journals."

"So it's really an ego hurt?"

"Not at all," she denied. "Implicit in the control of research is the method by which it will be conducted, the ultimate objective. That prevents the independently inclined investigator from pursuing the interesting little byways which so often show up during the course of research. Such byways often lead to the really great discoveries."

"Doesn't the government usually fund anything that looks promising?"

"Not unless it has a commercial or social value."

"So knowledge for the sake of knowledge is passé, is that it?"

"Very little knowledge is for the sake of knowledge," she replied. "Almost everything we learn has an eventual application. But on the whole you're right. It's part of our closed-loop thinking."

"You sound as if it's by design."

"It's the result of our limitations," she countered. "We might conjecture things far beyond our comprehension, but when we explore them we are forced to use known tools—the knowledge and research equipment we have at hand. Along with that, we move the subject from its incomprehensible state into the focus of our understanding, which makes it quite a new thing."

I listened, as fascinated by her fire and words as by what she was saying. What it added up to was that the incomprehensible was tailored so that it could be understood sufficiently well to investigate; by that time it no longer was the original problem, but one well within our purview.

She explained that the growing trend in that direction had shut the door to the really great mysteries of the universe—had encapsulated science in the nutshell of the Solar System in that it attempted to describe and explain the unknown in terms of what was known. "The same closed loop," she ended.

I eyed her curiously. "What do you think lies beyond the loop?"

"You asked that the first night," she chided. "I don't know."

"But you must. . . ."

"No," she cut in. She tossed her head disdainfully. "You'll have to forgive me if I'm bitter about government."

"Completely understandable," I assured her, and it was. Oh, the government was fine as far as the great majority of people were concerned. With paternal solicitude, it nourished them from birth to death. It guaranteed every child an education commensurate with his capabilities. It cared for the medically indigent, pensioned the elderly, and provided a guaranteed living-wage to each adult, regardless of circumstances. It also allowed a maximum of freedom, probably more than any people had ever enjoyed. A person could travel as he pleased, hold his own beliefs, say or do much as he chose. As long as he didn't act against the government.

That was the kicker.

Huge, monolithic, the government long since had abandoned its role as the servant of the people to assume that of the benevolent master. When it had, it had taken steps to make itself unassailable. Not that it was completely a matter of law. A person who criticized the government, even mildly, was apt to find his security clearance cancelled so that he couldn't work in any organization having commerce with the government. Inasmuch as that included practically every business, industry, and educational insti-

tution on Earth, it was tantamount to sentencing him to life
at the guaranteed minimal subsistence level. That provided
bread, a roof, and little else.

And people simply vanished.

I wouldn't whisper that, even to Ann, but it was the kind
of thing a person in my position came to know. People who
were too overtly critical, either by word or deed, had the
nasty habit of disappearing from the public view, never to
be seen again. The rumor, which I knew to be true, placed
such control actions under a secret section of the BPS,
the Bureau of Public Safety. The section even had an
ultra-secret code name: Department L. I wouldn't admit
my knowledge of that to anyone.

Not that the government of the Americas was any worse
than the autocracy that ruled Europe or the People's
Comintern that controlled Asia; they were all somewhat of
a mold. The one thing in their favor was the absolute
abolishment of war. There hadn't been a major conflict in
over two centuries. Pure survival, in an age when man
could annihilate a planet, had determined that. Yet the
shadow of war remained—a pot kept simmering to justify
the controls needed to unify a people and keep their attention diverted outward. All of which had little to do with
her complaint, but it did point up the system. There was
nothing she could do about it. I said so.

"I know." She forced a smile. "You mentioned Cairo.
What were you doing there?" I recognized the switch as a
device to close the door on that particular conversation. It
was a technique she used whenever we veered too close to
the subject of her work, or of her personal life or beliefs.
Her barriers were tall.

Reluctantly I told her of Cairo.

On one other occasion I came close to reaching her, to
understanding some of what she believed. As I recall, we'd
attended the theater and afterward were having cocktails.
Sitting across from me, the candlelight dancing on her
face, she was especially enchanting.

Musingly she'd asked, "Have you ever read Krado
Fromm?"

"His *Stellar Origin of Man?*" I had to smile. A twenty-first century philosopher, Fromm had made a big splash in his day with the theory that the human race first had evolved on a planet of another star. The theory had been put forth earlier, perhaps many times, but most had thought of the crossing as that of life spores. Like the Polynesian longboats of old riding the tides, such spores had ridden the radiation currents of space to seed the planets in their path—that was the general thesis. Fromm had seen man as the survivor of some cataclysmic disaster in which only a mere handful had reached Earth. The sensational aspect was that he'd pinpointed the star of man's origin, but with no factual evidence that I could recall. Fromm had extended his theory to explain the sudden appearance of the Cro-Magnon, the forerunner of modern man, who seemingly had come out of nowhere to eliminate the brutish Neanderthaler near the end of the last glaciation. The whole thing seemed quite implausible. I said so.

"Yet the early Martian explorers found human artifacts on the plains of Syrtis Major," she remonstrated.

"Human?" I arched my eyes.

"Artifacts from an intelligent form of life," she corrected. "At least it gives some support to Fromm's theory that others from the same disaster perhaps landed there."

"A few chunks of metal on a desert where nothing rusts," I commented. "They could have been from an early probe."

"Shaped chunks of metal," she corrected, "and we're quite certain they weren't from a probe."

"What does that mean?"

"We aren't alone in the universe."

"I hope it's not as crowded as Earth," I observed. That closed the conversation.

When I finally wangled a visit to her home, it was the blunt, frontal approach that did it. While driving back from supper at Malibu, I said, "I'd like to visit your bailiwick, see where you roost."

She sat straighter, looked up through the bubble-top at a

swath of glittering stars. Off to the right, curling combers, tinged with a green phosphorescent glow, crashed and pounded the white sand. It was a tense moment. "All right," she said finally.

I allowed her to guide me through the steep coastal hills, up to the cantilevered house that perched like a nightbird against the sky. It was smaller than I'd thought, but beautifully, if simply, furnished. The walls, paneled in imitation oak, held several striking paintings. Two sides of the main room were lined with shelves of books; a stone hearth dominated a third.

The layout of the adjoining doors suggested a bedroom, bath and kitchen. She didn't bother to show me through but led me upstairs to a single, large attic room that occupied all of the upper floor. Several comfortable appearing but well worn couches, a rack containing half a dozen musical instruments, a painter's easel, another large shelf of books—my eyes took them in with a sweeping glance. The wall-to-wall carpeting, designed for a putting green, appeared quite appropriate. I did not see the violin.

"I do most of my living here," she explained. I could see why. Opposite the small window I'd observed from the road, a glass wall on the canyon side afforded a magnificent view of the rolling hills beyond. The spectral glare of Los Angeles washed low against the sky. The contrast between the flood of light and the house-covered ridges notched against it, brought a feeling of complete isolation.

A sliding glass door opened onto a small veranda. Jutting out over the canyon, it reminded me of the poop deck of an ancient Spanish galleon. I wondered if that was where she stood when she sent her haunting melodies wafting through the hills. Or were they directed toward the stars? I can't say why that question occurred, except that it did.

While she busied herself with coffee, I opened the glass doors and stepped outside. The lights from surrounding houses lay like fireflies below me. The sky above was ebony, star-filled. The light, thundering down into my consciousness, dwarfed me, made me feel unutterably in-

significant. Yet it filled me with wonder, contemplation—
the curious elation the human animal gets when confronted
with the unknown. I speculated that of all nature's wonders, none had gripped man's imagination so much as the
sky. Seafarer, shepherd, explorer, wanderer—all have
contemplated it in silent awe. It is the last frontier. Only
the city dweller, caught in his hive, is immune to its gran-
deur.

I looked at the dark gully that fell away beneath me, at
the peaked roof-line silhouetted against the sky, at the
harsh, brittle light that stormed down from the heavens.
The house, the view, the sense of complete solitude—everything was magnificent. I told her so when she returned
with the coffee.

"My escape hatch," she answered.

"Escape from what?"

"The humdrum." We sat on the couch with our cups.

"Is life that boring?" I asked.

"Not really, but I enjoy the solitude."

"I can see its virtues," I admitted. "I've never really
known it myself." And I hadn't. My entire life, it seemed,
had been centered around people, activities. My world was
man-created. But that's the journalist's lot: the hive is his
habitat. I said so.

She nodded sympathetically. "You've missed something,
Joel."

"Time enough when I'm old."

"You must spend considerable time reading. It's amazing
how many fields you cover."

"Not in depth," I admitted. "Usually I just scratch the
surface. That's all the reader wants; or perhaps I should
say, the *Solar Press* readers. Most are not exactly intel-
lectuals."

"Don't undersell yourself," she reprimanded. "I've read
some of your interpretative work in the scientific as well
as the socio-economic and other fields. You appear to have
unusual insights."

"I'm surprised that an astrophysicist would read that
rag."

"I try to keep up with things."

"That should be easy."

"Why do you say that?"

I smiled. "It's a closed loop, remember. There's not too much to learn." She had to laugh. I asked impulsively, "Why don't you play for me?"

Her eyes strayed to the rack of instruments.

"The violin," I urged. She hesitated, then crossed slowly to a cabinet, opened it and drew out the instrument. She returned to the glass doors, opened them and looked up at the stars. Limned against the distant glow of the city, her face held a strange, pensive expression.

She lifted the instrument to her shoulder, tucked it under her chin and tuned it. Lingering on the steel "E" string, she drew out the high, plaintive note I'd heard from the road. It reverberated from the canyon walls. Gazing into the night, she began to play.

The music was low, sorrowful, haunting, with the strange quality of having originated from afar. It seemed borne in on a wind rather than having originated from the instrument tucked under the girl's chin.

I don't pretend to understand music, perhaps because my ears have become so jaded from what passes as music over the triscreen. But I know that certain pieces, mainly classical, touch me emotionally. Mozart and Tchaikovsky are cases in point. And the superb orchestrations of Karnelian, the twenty-first century genius. I also know that the violin requires a superb player to do it justice. She qualified easily.

I couldn't place the piece, and was certain I'd never heard it before. It was suggestive of remoteness, solitude, a vast sweep of emptiness. I visualized a white albatross high above a tropic beach, the footprints of a solitary camel in the Sahara sands, a firmament that held but a single star. It was the cry of a soul alone.

"The violin whispers of things beyond"—her words came back. Now I knew what she'd meant, yet there was no way to describe it. A feeling? An emotion? It was neither of those, yet neither was it purely a cerebral response. It

went far beyond that. It touched the . . . soul? But never mind; I knew how she felt.

The music ended and she turned slowly, her face rapt with an expression I couldn't interpret. Melancholy, yes, yet it also held something of a glory that was past my comprehension. She held the violin loosely at her side. I don't believe she even saw me. The tableau held for a good ten seconds.

"Beautiful," I murmured huskily. I stepped toward her and my arms went around her. I kissed her tenderly, then with more ardor. For a moment she yielded, straining against me before she tore her lips away.

"No, Joel," she cried. She stepped back, and looked mutely at the violin.

"I have no apologies," I said.

Her eyes came up to meet mine. "You'd better leave now."

"I have to drive you back to your car."

"Yes, I'd forgotten." She replaced the violin, slipped on a coat and accompanied me downstairs. We drove back to town in silence. When we reached her car, I held the door for her until she was seated. She started the engine, then rolled back the bubble-top and looked at me. "Good night, Joel."

Lightly, I kissed her cheek, drew back, and watched her drive away. The taillights receded in the darkness and vanished around a corner. I glanced at the stars, and for a moment fancied I heard the lonely cry of a violin. Another two months passed before I saw her again.

That was around the time I first met Mark Randall.

THREE

The face of Harvey Sinclair, editor-in-chief of the *Solar Press,* came to life on the visaphone screen. Heavy-jowled and swarthy, he scowled. Not that he was unpleasant; he wasn't. But he wore his moods in a way that enabled me to read him like a book. The book said the scowl was defensive because he was prepared to con me.

His small eyes bored out at me. "Mark Randall's slated to attend a science symposium at UCLA next week," he explained. "I'd like you to do an in-depth profile on him."

My mind automatically ticked off the fact that Sinclair seldom bothered with such trivia; the bait was far too small. Neither did it capture my own imagination. To my way of thinking, such an event was like spending an afternoon in a morgue. But something had caught Sinclair's attention.

"What's it about?"

"The ultimate nature of matter," he replied smoothly. It was his conning voice. "You'd better brush up on your atoms and quasi-stellars."

"Why not Bert Arvid?" I objected. Arvid, SP's top science reporter, had covered Randall extensively in the past.

"I'd like you to do it," insisted Sinclair. His eyes, flat and blank, told me he was withholding something.

"Any particular reason?"

"I want it slanted toward the man rather than his science," he explained. "His habits, motivations, beliefs— things like that. The human element, Joel."

"That doesn't answer the question."

"He's our top scientist, Joel."

"That still doesn't answer it."

"I have an inkling he might make big news one of these days," he admitted. His tone was too bland.

"On the ultimate nature of matter?"

"*Big* news, Joel."

I considered his emphasis. Harvey Sinclair's so-called inklings came through pipelines that extended into almost every level of government, business, and society in general, both on this world and beyond. In the position to give millions of dollars worth of free publicity at the nod of a head, he made it pay off. And it did. Very little of major importance failed to reach his ears in time to give him the edge on the competition.

I tried a frontal attack. "What kind of news?"

"I can't say, Joel." He could, of course, but his unwillingness to say, at least over the visaphone, told me his information had come from a source that demanded absolute anonymity. That wasn't unusual. By the same measure, it indicated the story could be very big indeed.

"Know where he'll be staying?"

"The Wilshire Sky Tower," he informed me.

"I'll have to cancel out on Buenos Aires."

"Buenos Aires can wait," Sinclair grunted. The phone clicked in my ear. As I watched his image fade from the screen, I had another thought: Ann Willett undoubtedly would attend the symposium. I could stretch out the assignment and cover Mark Randall in his native habitat. That would give me a good excuse for seeing her again.

I turned my attention to Mark Randall.

The conversation with Sinclair intrigued me. As a scientist, Mark Randall stood tall above his fellow colleagues. He was the Einstein of the twentieth century, the Wurlitzer of the twenty-first. His domination of the twenty-third-century world of science was complete. That generally was accepted.

Specifically, he'd probed deeper into the atom than any other man, had created a mathematical model that extended a dozen steps further yet. At the other end of the spectrum—"which really was the same thing," Mark Randall once said—he'd untangled the final mysteries of the quasi-stellars, those gigantic bombs of radioactive matter that hover in the remote fastnesses of the universe. In so doing, he'd taken a colossal step toward explaining how stars are born, the shape of the cosmos; he had painted the life and death of galaxies, made them appear as ephemeral as the buds of spring, and perhaps they are. It wasn't just in nuclear and astrophysics that Mark Randall was famed; he excelled in a dozen other fields as well.

But Harvey Sinclair, I knew, wasn't concerned with atoms or quasi-stellars; he had something quite different in mind. What? I recalled what I knew of Randall. He headed half a dozen or so scientific advisory boards; his name was on the masthead of several leading science journals; he was "Mr. Big" of the government's "think" factories.

That was one Mark Randall. Another was the Mark Randall who was deeply involved with the phenomenon of man himself. He'd published several widely acclaimed philosophical tomes on the nature of man, his destiny, his reason for being; he'd also published a psycho-medical exposition on the brain as the house of the mind. Deep stuff, but it wasn't the stuff that had put Harvey Sinclair on the scent. Sinclair's pursuit of sensationalism was of a different cut.

What was he after? Although I hadn't the remotest idea, I surmised it was something quite unrelated to any scientific achievement. That didn't tell me much. I could grab a nucjet to New York, pin Sinclair to the mast, but I reasoned it would be useless. Besides, Sinclair hadn't asked me to dig out *the* story, but merely to supply a good profile of the man for use when the story, whatever it was, did break. I'd have to take it from there.

The interview was easily arranged. I'd expected it would be. Usually it was the man low on the ladder who made interviews difficult, a tactic to boost dwarfed egos. Mark Randall didn't need that.

My first impression of him, when he opened the door to his suite in the Sky Tower, momentarily startled me. I'd seen numerous pictures of him, of course. The deep-set eyes in the craggy face, the hawkish nose, the shock of flaming hair—all that was quite familiar. But I wasn't quite prepared for the size of the man. I don't count myself a midget. I stand a shade better than six feet and tip the scales at around 180, but I felt like a midget compared to the man confronting me. Towering a good five inches above me, he was broad of shoulder, muscular, with the slim hips of a dancer. He had the movements of a cat. Power and grace were the words that struck me. I placed his age at close to mine—a few years on the sunny side of forty.

"I'm Mark Randall," he said. His hand shot out. I gripped it, murmured my name and followed him inside. He waved toward a couch and sat across from me. "What exactly can I do for you, Mr. Blake?"

"I'm interested in a profile for the *Solar Press*. I mentioned that." I weighed him. "Also, any special views or interests you might have."

"Nothing special."

"Mind if I use a tape?"

"Not at all." He smiled. "A great device to keep us from thinking."

"It's that," I agreed. I reached in my pocket and turned a switch. "I understand you're delivering the keynote address at the symposium."

"That, and presenting a paper." He nodded.

"On what topic?"

"The neutrino and anti-neutrino. Nothing really startling." He briefly described his subject, words that largely were wasted on me. As I got it, the neutrino and anti-neutrino approached that primordial something that constitutes the basic building-blocks of the universe. Sinclair would love that!

The talk gave me a chance to size him up. The eyes buried under the jutting orbital ridges were a brilliant cobalt blue, the lips thick, the mouth generously wide—a strong but not handsome face. It was far too rugged for that. One huge hand continually flexed and unflexed, as if it were the medium by which he released his thoughts. Deep and vibrant, his voice held a clarity that made each syllable a separate entity. He was considerate enough to define each word he believed might trouble me later on.

He finished abruptly. "Will that do it?"

"I can't say that I understood much of it," I confessed.

"How come they didn't assign Bert Arvid?"

"He'll probably cover the symposium," I explained. "Bert's our technical genius. I'm after a more personal profile."

"What good is that?"

I smiled. "You're news, whether or not you want to be."

"Shoot," he said. I questioned him about his background, boyhood, hobbies, why he'd decided to become a scientist. With that as background, I tackled his habits, motivations, beliefs. His responses were quick and, I believe, honest. Still, I wasn't getting at the core of the man. I was tending toward information that painted him blank, giving him the oblivion of the mass of humanity. In effect, I was fitting him into a slot. He knew it, too; his eyes held that kind of glimmer. I tried a new tack.

"You wrote a book about the brain as the house of the mind," I observed. "Wasn't that a departure from your usual interests?"

"I wouldn't say so."

"How might that tie in with the basic building-blocks of the universe?"

"I never claimed it did." He smiled.

"Not in so many words."

"You've read it?" His eyes were faintly puzzled.

"Not in depth. I couldn't follow it, but I did catch the glimmerings of ideas. Enough to intrigue me."

"Do you believe there could be a connection between the mind and the so-called basic building-blocks?"

"Possibly, I wouldn't know." I studied him. "Is there?"

"Not a direct relationship," he admitted. "But the brain is the instrument by which we conceive reality. By brain I'm including both the physical structure and the mind that inhabits it. Are they one entity or two? I believe we're speaking of a duality. Isn't it logical that we should strive to know how it works?"

"Do we?"

"Only superficially."

"The mind is what we make it," I observed. That was a bit of philosophy I dredged up from long ago.

"In a sense, yes, but in a greater sense it's how we use it. Its power is limitless."

"I was quoting"—I searched my memory—"from the early work of Charles Hedron."

"Hedron?" He was startled.

"I used to read him years ago. He was, as I recall, a neo-existentialist—believed that man was no more nor less than he was at any given moment. He saw man as a reactant to opportunity. . . ."

"You remember that?" Randall broke in.

"Fragments. I was quite young at the time. Later, when I wanted to read him again, I couldn't locate any of his books."

"Small wonder, Blake."

"Why do you say that?"

"It's of no importance." He shook his head impatiently and returned to the subject of the mind and how we conceive reality.

"What is reality?" I asked.

"Ah, that is the question." He stroked his chin. "What we call reality is only relative. I suppose I can put it that way. It's a concept, nothing more."

"Does that apply to physical states? A rock, for example —isn't that real?"

"In the ultimate, it's composed of atoms, the atoms of protons and electrons which in themselves are composed of subparticles ad infinitum, or so it would seem. Yes, the rock is real if you accept as reality an aggregate of trillions of trillions of particles, right down to units of energy which have no measurable mass. The rock is an object, solid, with a given density and weight, an apparent structure, but we really don't know what it is. What we call the reality of the rock is based on acceptance—the adherence to a certain blueprint, you might say—but not on absolute knowledge. There is very little that we know absolutely."

"Isn't that your goal, the discovery of the basic building-block . . . the ultimate nature of matter?"

"A step," he admitted.

"What lies beyond that?"

"The question of the *why* of things."

"Can we ever know?"

"A haunting question, Blake." He went to the window, gazed through a canyon formed of marching ranks of towering buildings that covered the coastal plain from mountain to sea. Small planes buzzed in the distance. He tilted his head skyward and asked, "Do you ever wonder about the universe?"

"Not in depth," I admitted. "The paradoxes throw me."

"So we accept them, is that it?"

"Have we a choice?"

He turned, the deep-set eyes focused and unmoving. I had the eerie impression that he was staring deep inside me—tracking the convolutions of my brain, watching it work. Later, in view of what transpired, I wondered that he had trusted me; later still I reasoned that the trust had come because of my casual reference to Charles Hedron, the philosopher whose works had disappeared. Still later. . . . But that's of no moment. What matters is that he did trust me, although I couldn't know it at the time. My only real awareness was of the brilliant cobalt-blue eyes that pierced me.

"Off-the-record?" His lips scarcely moved.

"If you wish it, yes."

"I believe there's much more to the universe than we suspect."

"In terms of life?"

"Yes, of course. An insensate universe would be quite incomprehensible, don't you think? I don't pretend to know the answers; I only suspect the outlines, but I'm certain there are other vistas."

"Reachable?"

"That is my hope."

"Are you speaking of other stellar systems?"

"Yes and no. I'm not speaking of time or space so much

as I am of human existence."

I remembered the conversation with Ann and asked, "Are you suggesting something like the old theory of Krado Fromm—that man's origin was stellar and that he came to Earth as a late-comer?"

He shook his head. "I believe Earth was the starting point."

"But how can. . . ." I stopped abruptly as his meaning suddenly became clear. "You're talking about vistas that exist in another time," I accused.

"Another time?" He contemplated it. "I prefer to think of time as a *oneness*. The tenses we use in speaking—must use to specify given parts of this oneness—give us our concept of time. In that sense the *past* and *present* are essential constructs."

"Is that a statement of fact, as you believe it to be, or a theory?"

He hesitated. "Haven't you ever had the feeling of déjà vu—of having seen all this before? I have that feeling about life as we know it, Joel—may I call you Joel?—that we've been here before."

"You're saying?" I stared wonderingly at him.

"That we're living in the backwash of our own history, yes."

"The word 'history' denotes the past."

"In the sense that we use it here," he agreed.

"Can you clarify your beliefs in terms of my understanding?"

"You mentioned the stars, Joel." He gestured upward. "I believe we're already there."

"Time travel?" My eyes must have mirrored my skepticism for a slight smile touched his lips. I asked, "You hope to contact some future vista, is that it?"

"The future to us, the present to them," he corrected.

"If your man of the future exists—if I might put it that way—and he's reached the stars, he must be advanced beyond all belief. If we accept your concept of time, and the ability to pierce it, why hasn't he attempted to contact us?"

"Do we know that he hasn't?" His eyes burned at me from the deep wells of their sockets and for an instant I had the impression of a man fanatical beyond all belief. But the impression faded as I studied his face. Calm, it held a certain sadness that reminded me of Ann.

"If such things are true, then what's the significance of our lives?" I asked.

"How do you mean that, Joel?"

"If this is a repeat performance, then we have to accept predestination. What would that do to self-initiative, motivation? What choice would we have but to follow the same old tracks? Was there another Joel Blake once, another Mark Randall? If so, we're nothing more than actors in a script. That would make it all seem quite futile."

"But need we follow the script? Suppose it were varied?"

I eyed him searchingly. "Then their future—I suppose I should call it their present—would be changed. That is, if we altered their past. . . ." I broke off to fumble with my thoughts. None of them quite made sense.

Mark Randall smiled. "It's worth considering," he said. "Perhaps Homo Superior—to give him a name—corrects the imperfections in his present by altering his past."

"How might they attempt it? Some sort of time capsule?"

He shook his massive head. "Through the mind, Joel."

"The mind?" I echoed.

"The human mind is the key to the universe, yet we know only the bare surface of it, the here and now. We live in the concept of the conscious self, see ourselves—when we think of it—as pygmies confined to a few motes of matter whirling blindly through a space-time continuum. We are locked in by our own concepts." He gestured airily. "The old existentialists used to tell us that man is what he is, that he is his own maker. In the ultimate that is true. But I say that right now he is his own warden. There are vistas beyond this one, Joel."

"Reachable only through the mind?"

"I believe so."

"Have you any tangible evidence?"

"Enough to convince me."

"What kind of evidence?"

He shook his head. "There are things I can't tell you. But that's enough; we've talked too much as it is."

"One more question," I insisted. "Are you doing research on such a project?"

"That answer's not for publication. None of this is."

"You have my word."

He asked, "Does the name Martin Wister mean anything to you?"

"Martin Wister?" Old memories stirred. "Wasn't he the famous neurophysiologist of several decades ago?"

Randall nodded. "He retired over a quarter of a century ago, at least as far as the public is concerned."

"He's still alive?"

"Very much so. He's in his nineties but functions like a man forty years younger."

"He's working with you on this?"

"We consult," he admitted hesitantly. I could understand his reluctance. If the government caught whiff of such a project, it would certainly take it over. I said so.

"That would end it," he agreed. "It would be buried in the never-never files."

"Why?"

"It would be dangerous."

"Because it might open a door?"

He nodded slowly, his eyes grave. "The government, all governments, fear the unknown, fear challenge. That is part of their survival reaction. When it comes to its own existence, a government wants only the status quo, the right to go on and on and on, with no change whatever. Oh, it speaks of change, but that's lip service. We explore the planets and satellites because we know they are devoid of intelligent life, that no risk is involved. Would we if we believed that somewhere out there was intelligent life? Never!"

I struggled with my thoughts, wondering again if perhaps Mark Randall hadn't stepped from that narrow balance we call sanity. Yet I knew he hadn't. Finally I asked,

"How does all this tie in with your attempt to discover the ultimate nature of matter? Such a discovery would add immeasurably to our knowledge, but would it free us in a physical sense? I'm thinking in terms of reaching your other vistas."

"Are we purely physical beings?"

"That is the unknown," I admitted.

"But need it be? That is the question." He relaxed again, sprawling out against the seat, his long legs extended. "However, I'm not so concerned with the ultimate nature of matter as with the ultimate nature of man. I'm certain that discovery won't be made in the laboratory but in the mind alone. The mind is the mystery, the window through which our parched souls look out on the universe around us. It is our tool of logic and conception—gives us reality as we know it. In that sense we create reality. That is why I called reality a relative thing, a concept. We accept that which we ourselves have conceived. We look but fail to see. Until we penetrate the veil. . . ." He shrugged.

"We go around and around like squirrels in a cage, is that it?"

"The analogy fits."

"Not mine," I confessed. "A girl I know voiced the idea. She believes that our senses, and therefore the cortex that feeds on them, are restricted—that we live in a closed loop from which there is no escape. She says we can't generate the momentum to break from our own particular orbit."

"An unusual girl, Joel. Did she suggest that the restriction was purposive?"

"That something in our nature caused us to lock ourselves in?"

"Something like that."

"I can't fathom what she really believes," I confessed. "She swims in deeper water."

"No clues to where she gets her ideas, eh?"

"From a violin," I said.

Randall grinned. "I'd like to meet that girl."

"Perhaps you will," I told him. "She's an astrophysicist

on the UCLA faculty. You'll probably meet her at the symposium."

"Dr. Willett?" He arched his brows.

"You know her?"

"Only through her work," he conceded. "She's an extremely advanced thinker."

"She's that." Even as I spoke, I realized I hadn't the slightest inkling of how Ann Willett's mind worked—to what heights or depths it traversed. I sensed, beyond her science, a touch of the mystical; or perhaps metaphysical is the better word. Her concern was with that which transcended the known. Yet she, like the flame-haired giant standing by the window, didn't believe the answer was to be found in the laboratory. It lay somewhere beyond, perhaps in the remote recesses of the mind itself; it lay waiting to be tapped. . . . I became aware of Randall's scrutiny.

"Tell me about the violin," he ordered quietly.

"It tells her things." In the quiet of the room, the statement didn't sound strange. As I continued, I had a vision of her profile limned against the distant glow of the city, saw the strange, pensive expression—heard again the plaintive, haunting melody that echoed through the canyons below. "It whispers of things beyond," I ended.

"Her words?"

I nodded.

"Many things are stimuli to thought, Joel."

"The music stirs her imagination."

"Not imagination." He shook his head impatiently. "Certain environments stimulate thought; they're like keys that open doors, allow the mind to roam. It's not the same for everyone, of course, but it's true. Dawn is my violin, perhaps because it's the moment of greatest solitude. For me, things hold greater clarity in that hour than in any other."

"The world stands still," I said.

"Yes, the world stands still." He nodded approvingly. We chatted a few moments longer but I quickly discerned that his mind no longer was on the interview. His eyes held a faraway look. Finally he glanced at his watch.

I took the cue and rose. "I appreciate your time."

"The pleasure has been mine, Joel." His face told me he sincerely meant it. "I hope we can get together again."

"The world is my beat. I'll give you a buzz next time I'm in Boston."

"Won't you be at the symposium?"

"Of course, but I imagine you'll have your hands full."

"Not that full," he said.

That night I sat in the darkness of my room to gaze out over the sea of lights that was Los Angeles. Behind me, spread out on the desk, was the profile I'd started on Mark Randall. I knew that I'd rip it up, start anew as I had half a dozen times already. Usually such profiles are comparatively easy, the form stereotyped so that they came out much as I wanted them the first time. But Mark Randall didn't fit the stereotype; there was no easy way to capture him.

Mark Randall the scientist, Mark Randall the philosopher, Mark Randall the mystic—which was the real Mark Randall? Or were they all one and the same man? Perhaps by dividing him into compartments I'd failed to grasp the totality of his being. Certainly he was the most complex man I'd ever encountered. But it went far beyond that. He was a stranger to me, to his fellow men. In some inexplicable way he walked alone. His wasn't an easy shell to crack.

I reflected on that. His answers had been honest, straightforward, yet baffling. Because of his belief that man lived in a time stream that was navigable? Certainly the concept revealed a vital part of him. He was a man on a search—a restless, prowling, inquisitive man driven by a brain powered by the fuel of curiosity. He had to know who and what he was, how he stood in relation to the universe. The primordial building-block he sought was complete knowledge. He was, in fact, much like Ann Willett.

"Dawn is my violin"—in those few words he'd acknowledged a kinship with her, had acknowledged the cry, the longing within her. I had the feeling that he understood her far better than I did, although he knew her only through her work, and from my brief words. Their chemistry was the same; they each walked alone.

I raised my eyes. Los Angeles is not the best place for viewing the night sky. The glow from its billion lamps washes out all but the brightest of stars. Still, I could discern faint pinpoints of light—enough to react to the vastness of that great gulf in which rode our lonely sun, accompanied by its small phalanx of planets, moons, comets, dust. Multiply our sun by a billion and you have a galaxy; multiply that by a billion and you have . . . what? Almost nothing when compared to the whole.

Time and infinity—what were they really? What was matter and what was life? The only overwhelming fact that I could draw was that I didn't know. The mere contemplation of such paradoxes made me feel akin to a single life-cell afloat in a primeval sea.

How could Mark Randall ever hope to know the true nature of the cosmos? That implied far more than the physical building-blocks themselves; it inferred the great questions of *how* and *why*. He was hurling himself straight at the monstrous dilemma posed by the nature of life. His challenge, at the least, was audacious.

Man was a pygmy, I reflected, yet Mark Randall refused to acknowledge that. He believed man to be far greater than we knew, that he long since had crashed the borders of this narrow reality in which we lived. More, he hoped to achieve that same crossing. How? The answer was beyond me.

Before I fell asleep I had another question: What was Harvey Sinclair's interest in Mark Randall? Perhaps I'd read too much into Sinclair's motives.

Somehow I didn't believe that.

FOUR

I didn't reach the symposium until the close of the first session. By then it was too late to introduce Mark Randall to Ann; they'd already met. When I arrived, they were standing outside Wurlitzer Hall engrossed in conversation with Bert Arvid, the science reporter. Their figures were caught in a shaft of sunlight.

I had the momentary impression that Arvid wasn't with them, that they stood alone—a flame-haired giant and his slender companion. It was as if the building, the broad steps leading to it, the fountain in front and the trees beyond had ceased to exist—that nothing remained except the two figures caught in the focus of my eyes. An absurd impression, perhaps, but one that was to come to me time and again in the years yet unborn. Neither did I wonder at what strange chemistry had brought them so swiftly together. It was the kinship of solitude. I could think of no other way to put it.

Ann saw me first. "Joel Blake," she exclaimed. A smile lit her face. Randall and Arvid turned.

My eyes went to the scientist. "See you've already met."

"Couldn't wait for you to get here," replied Randall. Ann laughed.

"Can't say that I blame you. What momentous thing did I miss, outside your keynote address?"

"Not a thing." Randall smiled. "It was quite dry and stuffy."

"It was not," declared Ann. Bert Arvid let one eye droop knowingly. Small and thin-faced, he had the sad look of a spaniel.

We chatted briefly before I asked, "What's next on the agenda?"

"That's it for today," answered Randall. "We meet in the morning to start our committee work."

"Lunch?" I asked hopefully.

He refused with a smile. "We've already been snared by several of our colleagues," he explained. I fancied I caught a fleeting look of regret in Ann's face, but couldn't be certain.

When they took their leave, Arvid said, "I didn't expect to find you here." The statement held a question.

"Harvey wants a nontechnical profile on Randall," I explained. "I wanted to see him in his native habitat. How about a sandwich?" Arvid nodded. We chose a small café near the campus.

Arvid sampled the coffee, smacked his lips and asked, "What do you think of him?"

"Mark Randall? He's quite a boy."

"An understatement," observed Arvid. "He's the genius of the age—perhaps of all ages. He's Newton and Einstein and Wurlitzer all rolled into one. No one in this day and age can even touch him. Have you interviewed him yet?"

"One session. Not enough to grab him."

"Think you ever will?"

"He's complex," I admitted. "Some of his ideas threw me."

"Oh?" He looked slightly surprised.

"I couldn't follow them."

"His research?"

"You might say." I tried another tangent. "He's certainly probing a new frontier."

"He mentioned that?"

I nodded noncommittally. "Not for publication, of course."

"I wouldn't breathe a word of it."

"Government?"

"They'd quash it right now, Joel."

"Why?"

He shook his head. "Don't ask me, Joel. I don't want to answer that."

"It can't be that much of a secret, Bert. Harvey Sinclair knows."

"He does?" His head jerked up.

"At least he's got an inkling. That's why he assigned me to do the profile."

"Probably a lot of people know about Mark's speculations. Scientists are prone to kick those things around among themselves. Politically they're quite naïve." He eyed me uneasily. "What exactly did Sinclair say?"

"He expects that Randall might hit the big news."

"I hope not!" Arvid appeared shaken.

"He didn't say why." I eyed Arvid speculatively, caught by his evasiveness. It wasn't like him. In the past we'd exchanged information quite freely. Sensing his withdrawal, I asked bluntly, "What's it all about, Bert?"

"You know as much as I do. You can draw your own conclusions."

"What conclusions?"

"Please, I don't want to talk about it. I wouldn't ever mention his ideas, Joel, not to anyone."

"Breaking the time barrier?" I asked quizzically. I was fishing and he knew it. When he didn't answer, I continued, "That idea's old, Bert. It's been pounded to death for centuries."

"Not by men of Mark's stature."

"You believe he has something?"

"I'm afraid to think."

"About what?"

He raised his head slowly, a sick look in his eyes. "Something frightening is happening to the world, Joel. It's enough to make a man think he's going crazy. It's, it's. . . ." He broke off, his gaze fixed on his plate.

"It's what?" I prompted.

"I don't know," he muttered. "That's the damnable part of it. I sense things that no one else seems to notice. At first I thought it was just me, that I was coming apart. But now. . . ."

"What kind of things?"

"I can't tell you, Joel, but I'm certain Mark Randall

knows. I'm certain he knows all about it. Not that I'd ask. I don't want to know. Some things are better left unknown. This is one of them."

"I can't subscribe to that, Bert."

"I can't help you." He straightened with effort. "We've talked too much. Take it from me, Joel, we really have. If I were you, I'd forget that we ever mentioned the subject. And don't object. I can see it in your face. The knowledge could be damned dangerous."

"To me?"

"To everyone who might know about it."

"Including Mark Randall?"

"Especially Mark Randall."

"Isn't that stretching it, Bert?"

"Not in this case," he answered harshly. We finished the meal in silence. I could understand his worry for Mark Randall, all right. If Mark stood to open the door into another world—or was it into another time?—the government would move heaven and hell to stop him. Karl Burger's secret Department L would see to that. But I couldn't quite see how the knowledge could be threatening to me. Department L might interrogate me, of course, but that would be about the extent of it.

"Something frightening is happening to the world"—what did Arvid mean by that? Probably it had been just a figure of speech. But I didn't think so. Bert Arvid wasn't a man to use the language lightly.

When I pondered the conversation later, I felt an odd excitement. Bert Arvid was the rare science reporter who took his work seriously. He'd delved deeply into the technical aspects of mathematics, physics, chemistry, physiology, and most of the other brain disciplines. If the truth were known, he probably was far more knowledgeable than many of the scientists he interviewed.

If Bert believed that Mark Randall was standing at some strange new threshold, that belief held weight. Yet how could time have a multiple nature? It could in the mind, of course. There the past and present and future were inextricably linked, constantly merging and separating until they all seemed one. But that was mental time. Yet did time hold any reality except that which was measured in the mind? As an abstract thing, it couldn't exist. Or could it?

I wished I'd quizzed Bert Arvid on that.

The symposium, as I had suspected, consisted of committee meetings, papers, dry discussions, all conducted in an atmosphere as quiet as that of a morgue. Yet, somehow, I sensed that it was explosive with activity. "A thought," it has been said, "is louder than a bomb." I had to admit that I was out of that league.

Since both Mark and Ann usually were caught in luncheon dates, they were fairly inaccessible. Not that I remained around much, but I did pop in and out at what I believed were appropriate moments. And occasionally we did find time to chat, which made it all worthwhile.

I didn't see Bert Arvid again. I didn't know why that perturbed me, but it did. Neither could I forget his worried advice, the sick look in his eyes when he told me something frightening was happening to the world. I wanted to ask Mark about it, but never quite found an opening.

At the close of the symposium I managed to beard Mark and Ann as they emerged from Wurlitzer Hall. "I'm in dire need of two guests for supper," I stated.

"Delighted," replied Randall, "if I might speak for Ann."

"Of course," she responded.

"Sevenish?"

"That would be fine," she assented.

As a special setting, at least one that greatly appealed to me, I chose one of the better marine restaurants located on the continental shelf in an undersea complex off the Malibu coast.

They were enchanted with my choice. Over cocktails we watched schools of sardines glide past the glass walls of our booth. Like ghosts they swam out from among the waving sea fronds into the emerald green water lit by the glow through the windows.

A solitary jellyfish eased past, raising and lowering the

edge of its umbrella in a steady rhythmical motion to propel it through the water. Idly I wondered from whence it came, to where it was going. Smaller than a thumbnail, it appeared a puny thing against the vastness of its setting.

"It looks so lonely," exclaimed Ann.

"All life is lonely," Mark Randall replied. I looked at him, and for a moment there was silence. I thought again of the lonely voice of the violin, the quiet freshness of the world at dawn. As I did, his meaning struck me. Life, no matter how proliferous, still rode a frail craft through an immensity in which man's loudest shout was less than a whisper.

I'd never thought of man as lonely until I considered him in that light. But then I could see it—man, an ephemeral incident in the stream of time. From that viewpoint, life seemed quite futile. I said so.

"Futile?" Mark eyed me speculatively.

"Are we more than that jellyfish?" I asked.

"What has that to do with futility?"

"If a person could be projected a billion light years out into space and there light a candle which as instantly would be extinguished, you would have a fair analogy of man's total existence," I explained. "At least that's how it strikes me. Man's like that brief flame, absolutely insignificant."

"He is?"

"When measured against time and infinity, yes."

"Your time and infinity," he corrected. "I don't hold that man is futile and insignificant. I believe that this universe is great because of him."

"That's not man as I know him!"

"We're looking at different parts of the scale, Joel."

"Ah, time again."

"If man were like your brief flame, there'd be no purpose to life," interrupted Ann.

I switched my gaze to her. "Is purpose a prerequisite?"

"Certainly."

"Why?"

"All life has purpose," she responded. "The problem is to discern it."

"What is the purpose of life?"

"To fulfill our destiny."

"What is our destiny?"

Mark laughed. "Aren't we talking in a circle? That question is unanswerable until we know the purpose of life."

Ann eyed me insistently. "Don't you believe life has a purpose?"

"Food, drink, the nightly opiate of the triscreen—that's the measure of human endeavor," I answered cynically.

"Not for everyone, Joel."

I shifted my eyes to Mark. "What is your concept of human destiny?"

"That is the great unknowable, Joel. We plan as we go, quite haphazardly, I might say." He gazed silently at a passing school of fish before continuing. "We are children groping in the night. The more we discover about the nature of the universe, the less we know, if only for the reason that we uncover ever greater paradoxes. The problem first rose when man began looking outward—wondering, questing, reasoning, inching his way toward what he hoped was the ultimate knowledge. Yet each discovery diminished our stature, dwarfed us. In a sense, we've sold ourselves down the river."

"How do you reason that?"

"We no longer see ourselves as being in an evolutionary process, but rather as creatures of stasis, in which we believe that all further advances will be purely technological. I'm speaking of the present viewpoint. We've conceived of the universe in a certain way and by so doing we've boxed ourselves in."

"The limits of our expansion appear self-evident," I observed.

"They do?"

"I'm certain of that. I'm not speaking of your temporal aspects, but of the universe as this particular Homo sapien sees it."

"Ah!" Mark smiled.

I said, "We know the Solar System rather well. Earth is

the only really habitable planet. On the others we have to create Earth environments—manufacture our oxygen, dome our communities or bury them beneath the planetary crusts, supply them from here. The next stop is Far Centauri, which you'll have to admit is rather a long leap. Even a time traveler would face that limitation."

"In the universe as we conceive it, yes."

"So we strike out for a new reality, is that it?" I shook my head. "Where would we start? How would we chart our course?"

"Every pioneer faces that question, Joel."

"That's the easy answer. It doesn't tell me anything."

"You start by looking inward," replied Mark. "The mind has created this reality. That's understandable, for the mind knows only what its senses tell it, and its sensory apparatus is extremely limited. Would you expect the universe to be circumscribed by the limits of those senses?"

"How do you conceive of it?"

"Life? I believe it has an existence which lies beyond our senses—beyond our self-imposed limitations of time and space."

"We have instruments that transcend our senses," I argued.

"True, but they're fashioned to extend our senses. We create the more powerful telescope and microscope, build ever more sensitive instruments, but we use them to discover more of what we already know. Our research at best is conventional and predictable and, I might add, designed for a three-dimensional universe." Mark eyed me soberly. "We need to break the pattern, Joel, take a new look."

"Is that what you're doing?"

He smiled faintly. "We've discussed that."

"I'm trying to clarify my thinking," I explained.

"I'm working in that direction," he admitted.

"What exactly do you hope to find?"

"Higher life forms."

"Alien?"

"Human, Joel, we're discussing human destiny."

"At another point in the time stream, is that it?"

"That's the general idea."

"Time," I stated wonderingly. "How can there be anything but the past, the present, the future, each discrete from the other? How can there be any reality other than the present?"

"That's a matter of viewpoint, Joel. Your expression, 'the time stream,' describes it. But is time an ever rolling stream, a steady progression from past to future? By the clock, yes, and by our subjective impressions. But that's because our subjective impressions are oriented to this reality, to this here-and-now, just as they are locked to the concept of a three-dimensional universe. I'm not denying that there is a present, but the present itself is a subjective matter, a conscious awareness. And what is subjective is quite unrelated to the true nature of things. But if we define the present as being a time of awareness, then the present is whenever and wherever such an awareness exists. If a conscious form of awareness exists in what we call our past or our future, then that past or future is the present to that life-form."

"Are you saying that the present can exist in the past or in the future?"

"To the conscious state, yes."

"That gives me an eerie feeling," I confessed.

"Why?"

"I feel like a fish in a gigantic bowl, an ant under glass. I can all but sense some super scientist staring down at us, saying 'Ah!' It's not a comfortable feeling."

"Man under glass." Mark chuckled. "Perhaps it's a better analogy than you know."

"You hope to penetrate time, that's what you're saying. But precisely how?"

"Through the mind. I've said that."

"But how? Some temporal type of teleportation?"

"It goes beyond that."

"Can you put it in words?"

"Not really." Mark shook his head.

"The idea is fantastic," I declared.

"Nothing is fantastic in this universe or any other, Joel."

"When do you expect to accomplish this?"

"Perhaps soon." As his glance traveled back to the waving sea fronds, I felt a stillness inside me. It was a stillness brought by the certainty of his belief. Now I knew why Harvey Sinclair had wanted the profile on Mark Randall; he knew that the flame-haired giant stood on the verge of some momentous discovery.

My mind reeled. Other worlds! Other universes! It seemed absolutely inconceivable. Momentarily I again wondered if the man weren't mad, or at least caught up in some mystical philosophy which had swept away the foundations of reason. I gazed mutely at Ann; her face revealed nothing.

I asked hoarsely, "This is true?"

"Quite true," he answered. His smile closed that particular conversation for the night. Ann broke in with an exclamation about the beauty of the undersea world. From then on the conversation was light; they kept it that way.

As we rose to leave, she suggested, "Shall we stop at my place for a pot of coffee?"

"That would be pleasant," said Randall. Too surprised to speak, I could only nod. The single time I'd seen the interior of the house was when I'd practically forced the invitation. Since, I'd learned well that Ann Willett valued her privacy above all else.

But I wasn't Mark Randall, I reflected ruefully. Although he'd never met her before the symposium, he'd managed to penetrate the shield of reserve she had never lowered for me. I had the feeling that the two were in perfect harmony, as if silent currents of understanding flowed constantly between them. I was the oddball of the party.

Normally I would resent such a situation, but not this time. Alongside Mark Randall, almost any man would stand in the shade. I could match him neither physically nor mentally. Few men, if any, could. And in the field of pure intellect, Ann Willett also dwarfed me. That was difficult to acknowledge, but true.

As we returned along the coast, I rolled back the bubble-top to allow the cool breeze to brush our faces. To our left a star-filled sky reached down to touch the sea. Giant green combers curled and crashed against the white beach. A sibilant hiss filled the air as the waters rushed down the sand slopes to collide with the incoming breakers. A magnificent night.

But I wasn't thinking of that; I was caught with Mark Randall's beliefs. How could another universe or universes exist in the same space-time continuum, yet remain undetected? He hadn't said the same space-time continuum, of course, but reason dictated that it had to be that way. A universe (plural?) that couldn't be seen by telescope or microscope, that couldn't be detected by the most powerful laboratory instruments—was that possible?

If Mark Randall's revelations had startled me, not so Ann. Throughout the entire conversation she had exhibited no surprise, no air of question. When I considered it, I realized his ideas in many ways touched on her own. Both saw man as a creature of self-exile in a box of his own creation. Their complete rapport made me feel more of an outsider than ever.

I turned in from the coast and drove in along the winding road to the lonely house that perched like a nightbird against the sky. Ann led us upstairs to the den, flicked on the lights, then went down to the kitchen to put on the coffee.

As Randall surveyed the shelves of books and racks of musical instruments, it was clear that the action was purely mechanical; his face held a faraway demeanor that told me he was deep in thought. He scarcely seemed to realize I was there.

Finally he opened the glass doors and stepped out onto the veranda. Limned against the spectral haze cast by the city lights, he presented a solitary figure. He held an air of aloofness. Not consciously, for that wasn't in his nature. But it was there all the same, the impression of a man who stood apart from his kind.

In that moment I had the wild idea that he wasn't human

at all, but was a step above it—a new Cro-Magnon contemplating his world. There was something magnificent in the reflection, but also chilling. Idly I wondered how the Neanderthaler had felt when first he'd confronted his successor. Almost immediately I had to smile; I knew exactly how he'd felt.

Randall tilted his head to gaze upward at the sky. For a long moment he held the pose, as if his gaze had riveted on a particular point of light that he was examining minutely. I wondered what he saw there. Or was I letting my imagination run riot? Had it been anyone but Mark Randall. . . . But it was Mark Randall; that was the whole point.

He turned as Ann came back with the coffee. "Magnificent," he exclaimed. He gestured toward the dark hills notched against the sky.

"Too many neighbors," she replied.

"Yet you have solitude."

"Not enough." She spoke lightly, with a meaning that eluded me. But not Randall. He nodded understandingly, a gesture that seemed to convey a torrent of words. I felt that a high wall had shut me out. It wasn't that way when I was with either of them alone, but together they formed a unit against the world. Perhaps, as later I was to think, against the universe.

While we chatted over coffee, mostly about inconsequential things, I sensed an undercurrent, as if some subliminal conversation was occurring between them. Idiotic, of course, but that's how I felt. Mark seemed to understand, for he deliberately slanted questions my way, listening attentively as I answered. But the undercurrent still remained.

Finally Ann lowered her cup, went over to the cabinet and drew out the violin. This time I felt no surprise. We watched quietly as she walked to the edge of the veranda to stare upward at the stars for a long moment before tucking the instrument under her chin. She tuned it, gazed out into the night, and began to play.

Again the music was plaintive, haunting, with the strange quality of having originated from afar. It was not the piece that she had played before, but another. I glanced at Randall. His face, absolutely immobile, held an intense concentration.

Of one thing I was certain: Whatever language the instrument spoke, Mark Randall understood. But not I. The music brought an imagery that stirred my imagination, but that was all. Nor could I have described the imagery, for it was as elusive as a minuet in color, with neither substance nor geometric proportion. Any meaning it might have escaped me entirely.

Abruptly she ceased playing and lowered the instrument. For a long moment she looked into the night before turning. When finally she did, her face held a strange, melancholic expression. Her eyes, like Randall's, looked not at this world. Or was that my imagination?

Neither of us stirred as she replaced the violin. When she turned back to face us, Randall rose. "Thank you," he said quietly. I started to add my own praise, but stopped. Randall had said everything there was to be said. Their eyes met briefly before she transferred her gaze to me.

"It's been a pleasant evening," she said.

"Extremely pleasant," Randall broke in, "but it's time we're leaving."

"Perhaps we can get together again," I suggested.

"I'll be on the Coast for a few more days," he said.

I grinned. "This business is too unpredictable to plan from one day to the next, but I certainly hope to see you before you leave."

As it turned out, I didn't. When I arrived home, I found a recording message in the visaphone requesting me to call the New York office first thing in the morning. I knew what that meant: Harvey Sinclair had waxed hot on Buenos Aires again.

From Buenos Aires my assignments took me to Rio de Janeiro, by nucjet to Cape Town, and finally to Sicily to attend the dedication of an undersea complex in the emerald waters off Palermo. It was a routine run, the kind I usually enjoyed. This time my pleasure was marred by not being able to pursue my friendship with Mark Randall. Certainly he was the most extraordinary man I'd ever met, and the most puzzling. At least I had ample time to think about him.

Aside from that, I couldn't rid my mind of the things he'd told me. Unseen universes that existed simultaneously in the past, present, and future! Man, the prime mover of the cosmos! That's what it amounted to. That was the stuff of mystics and dreamers and science fiction writers, only Mark Randall fitted none of those categories. Neither did Ann Willett.

One other thing lay heavy in my mind. Mark Randall had cautioned me that his work was not for publication, yet Harvey Sinclair, I was certain, had knowledge of it. Perhaps it bothered me because of the air of secrecy Sinclair had imparted when requesting the profile. Or was it because of Bert Arvid's reaction?

I stewed over the possibilities for most of the trip. When I reached Los Angeles I started to call Ann, saw it was midnight, then caught a cab to my apartment and fell into a troubled sleep.

From a stand in the lobby next morning, the headlines of the *Solar Press* screamed: FAMED SCIENTIST MISSING! Dazed, I felt as if the floor suddenly had dropped from under me. I felt sick as I bought a copy. Mark Randall's face, taken from an angle that gave it an inquisitive expression, stared out at me. My eyes jumped to the black type.

Mark Randall, dean of American scientists, today was sought by police following his sudden disappearance. . . . I read to the end, an account that told little except that Randall had been discovered missing following his failure to attend an important seminar on astrophysics, which he had been scheduled to conduct at the Massachusetts Institute of Technology. His modest Cambridge home had revealed no sign of foul play. There was more of the same.

The story perturbed me. Why a widespread search for a man who had been missing but a few hours? Worse, his disappearance had been announced by Karl Burger, director of the Bureau of Public Safety. What had the BPS to do with a case which, on the face of it, was purely a matter for the local police? That was damning. Aside from that, the wording gave the impression that Randall somehow was guilty of something. The story didn't state that, but it was the kind of thing a sharp reader would catch—sort of journalistic double-talk that I knew to be intentional. Why?

My eye caught the profile I'd done on Randall. Sinclair had placed it on the front page. As I began to read, I did a double take. *His eyes, a brilliant cobalt blue, held a wild look that made me uneasy*—the words fairly screamed at me. Shocked, I read them again. My God, I'd never written a thing like that!

I hurriedly scanned the rest of the column. Here and there my words had been changed, innuendoes implanted to give the impression that Mark Randall was highly unstable. By the time I finished, my hands were shaking. That the changes had been purposive, I knew. Someone, somewhere, was starting to downgrade Mark Randall's image, tear him from his pedestal to make him more vulnerable to attack. That trick reached back to the days when they wrote on papyrus.

Bert Arvid's warning flooded back into my mind. As I hurried to my apartment, I tried to sort out the implications. Was the government trying to block Randall's research? That seemed indisputable. No monolithic self-preserving government would allow the opening of a door to a power immensely greater than itself.

But why destroy the man? That indicated haste, a desperation, a something-that-had-happened that had given the government no time to apply the normal pressures. Had Mark made contact? Or did the government suspect the imminence of it? Either event would explain Karl Burger's personal interest in the case. The BPS! I shivered. I hoped that didn't translate to mean Department L! That possibility did scare me.

In less than thirty seconds after I'd placed my call, Harvey Sinclair's heavy-jowled face came to life on the screen. The defensive look in his eyes didn't escape me.

"Who changed my profile on Mark Randall?" I demanded angrily.

"Now Joel. . . ."

"They make him sound like a madman!"

"Please, Joel, listen."

"You'd better make it good," I grated harshly. Harvey Sinclair might be my superior but I was sufficiently well known to catch an equally good job elsewhere and I knew he knew it.

"There were only a few small changes. . . ."

"Please!" I interrupted. I gave him a pained look.

"It's not something that I care to discuss . . . now."

I started to answer, then stopped. The *now* was the cue. It told me that Sinclair believed his phone was tapped. On that basis I went along with him. "I thought perhaps some subordinate had done it," I said.

"No, it's just that I thought you missed the slant on him, Joel. It's policy to portray a man in his true perspective, you know."

"Well, sure, if I muffed it."

"I believe you did, Joel."

"I'm sorry." I smiled weakly into the visaphone. "I'll try to do better next time."

"Just say that Mark Randall concealed his true colors," Sinclair replied airily. He made a few remarks concerning my next assignment before the screen went blank. I felt a touch of fear as I watched his image fade into nothingness. Harvey Sinclair was a powerful man and, within reason, an ethical one. At least I'd always found him to be. Yet, he'd deliberately set out to destroy the world's greatest scientist. His words told me that the innuendoes in the story were nothing compared with what was to come.

My God, would Ann believe I did it? The possibility shook me, left me cold all over. Perhaps she'd assign it to jealousy! I desperately wanted to call her, but glanced at the clock and realized I hadn't time. I had to move fast.

Within the hour I was on a nucjet headed for New York.

FIVE

Harvey Sinclair was hunched over his work when I entered his office. His massive shoulders fell away into a plumpness that shouted of his sedentary occupation. He gave no sign he heard me. "What's it all about?" I barked. He jerked up his head, startled.

"Shhhh!" A finger shot to his lips. I gaped at him. Did he actually believe his office was bugged? Suddenly I knew that he did, and that probably it was. That jolted me.

I managed to say, "I stopped in to talk over the assignment you mentioned."

"Glad you did, Joel." His voice held a false heartiness. As he rose and came around the end of the desk, I caught the shadow of fear in his face. It must have transmitted itself to me, for suddenly I had the sensation of a thousand hostile eyes on me. It wasn't pleasant.

I fought down my uneasiness and remarked, "You're looking well."

"All work and no play," he replied. We made small talk while he steered me into an adjoining washroom. He closed the door, turned on the water and flipped his hand through it to create a splashing sound. The elaborate precautions made me nervous. With his lips pressed to my ear, he whispered, "Know anything about Randall's whereabouts?"

I shook my head.

"Don't mention his name until we're out of here," he breathed. I signified that I understood.

"How about lunch? I can't stand that stuff they serve on the nucjets."

"A sandwich," he agreed. "I'm on a diet." He slipped on a jacket and we went down to the street. Conscious of remote pickups, I held my questions in check. But my

54

thoughts ran rampant. I could understand Bert Arvid's fright; timidity was his nature. That didn't apply to Harvey Sinclair. It wasn't like him to soft-pedal it for anyone, let alone know the fear that I had glimpsed in his face. If he were frightened, it was for good reason. That knowledge wasn't reassuring.

He led me to a small café, chiefly notable for a triscreen that blared little but raucous music. It was a poor place to eat but a good place for private conversation. At least the whispers could be drowned in the noise spectrum.

He chose a booth directly under the amplifiers. When we'd placed our orders, he said rather loudly, "Let me tell you about this girl I met. You'll love it." Leaning forward, he added in the barest of whispers, "For God's sake, don't mention Mark Randall."

"Some gal," I snickered. "Tell me more."

"Department L." He scarcely breathed the words. Department L! I froze. The department in charge of vanishing people! The very name was a death knell. Small wonder Harvey Sinclair was frightened. Few men knew of the department's existence; fewer still failed to tremble at the hint of the name. Yet the revelation didn't surprise me. Somehow I had expected it, probably as a result of Bert Arvid's warning. Not that it lessened the shock.

I gazed at him across the table. For all his power, he could be brushed aside like a gnat. The same applied to me. Now I knew why he'd changed my column; he'd been ordered to. It was that simple.

Despite his reluctance to talk, I knew I had to push him. I also had to dispel the fear that had gathered in my own mind—fear for Mark Randall. All at once that fear was starkly clear. Leaning toward him, I whispered, "Have they grabbed him?"

"Not yet." He shook his head. "He's running fast."

"Did he make contact?"

"Contact?" His puzzled frown told me he knew nothing of Mark Randall's hopes or beliefs. He was merely following orders. But it would be that way. Department L wouldn't confide the real reason for its persecution. Why should it when it wasn't answerable to anyone other than Karl Burger?

"What have they got on him?" I murmured. I could all but see him juggling his thoughts, trying to come up with an answer that would placate me while telling me nothing at all. It was there in his dark eyes—the indecision and speculation.

Finally he said, "He's been misappropriating government funds, using them for illegal research."

"Nonsense," I snapped.

"Shhhh!" He blanched.

"Then tell me the truth," I demanded.

"I don't know, Joel." His eyes pleaded with me. "So help me, that is the truth."

"You know something!"

He glanced furtively around before leaning closer. "He's discovered something that's dangerous to the government, Joel. That's all I know. Now for God's sake, don't push it, please. We'll both have Department L on our necks."

The frightened look on his face told me he was truthful. That he didn't know more than that made sense; the government moved in wondrous ways that few of its participants understood, let alone an outsider. Secrecy was the great code word. For all his pipelines, on this particular story Sinclair was on the outside looking in. He was a pawn in a game of queens. He knew that Randall was in hot water, but not why. I decided against telling him.

One thing seemed clear: Either Mark Randall had established contact with his mysterious universe, or was on the verge. In either event the government had caught wind of it, was reacting out of what must have been almost panicky fear. Department L wasn't out to capture Mark; it was out to kill him.

Sinclair raised his voice. "I can't tell you her name, Joel. She's too well known."

I laughed dutifully. "How about my assignment?"

"I thought I'd let you rove on your own, see what you can come up with."

"I'd like that." I smirked. That was exactly how I had been operating for nearly ten years.

"Pick your subject, run it down, see what makes it tick," said Sinclair. "I know you'll do a good job."

"Sounds great," I replied. I knew exactly what he was saying. Harvey Sinclair was scared stiff but he still wanted to know what the Randall affair was all about. It was a case of his training overriding his discretion, for which I was grateful. At the same time, he was telling me that I was on my own, that if I stumbled I would stumble alone. That was fair enough. It at least gave me a free hand with all expenses paid.

A chilling thought struck me. Since Sinclair had known before the symposium that Mark Randall was in the broth, it stood to reason that the BPS had known. Or, to be more exact, Department L. That undoubtedly meant that Randall had been under surveillance during the period of his friendship with Ann. That could place her in real jeopardy. The prospect was unnerving.

I leaned across the table and asked Sinclair how he had known about Randall beforehand.

"Tipped." His lips silently formed the word. I knew better than to ask the identity of the tipster; he wouldn't give that information to his own mother, nor could I blame him.

While we finished our meal, I contemplated the possibilities. None of them was overly cheerful. One was that I was under surveillance due to my association with Mark Randall. A second was that Ann was under surveillance for much the same reason. A third was that Ann's friendship with Randall had progressed to a point where they might grab her to hold as bait, or treat her as an accomplice. That last gave me the shakes.

I had one more question. "Does Bert Arvid know anything about this?" I asked.

His eyes grew speculative. "Should he?"

"Bert's covered him a lot. They were quite close."

"I don't know," he breathed. "I don't want to know."

"Just as well," I agreed. I'd known the answer before-hand, of course, but I'd wanted to ascertain the degree of Bert's involvement. Apparently his information had de-rived from a separate source.

Sinclair drained his coffee cup, set it down, and asked, "Going back tonight?" Translated, the words meant: Get out of town! It also meant that he didn't want me around to ask embarrassing questions.

"Booked on an early flight," I assented.

"Keep in touch."

I caught his eye. "If you don't hear from me in quite a while, I might be in a strange place."

"Yeah," he replied dolefully. I smiled as cheerfully as I could. We made small talk while we walked back to the office. There I bid him adieu and made my arrangements to return to the Coast.

I was leaving when I glimpsed Bert Arvid entering the lobby. He tried to pretend he hadn't seen me but I caught his arm. "What's happening?" I whispered.

"For God's sake, Joel."

"Yeah, I know, the building's bugged. But answer me or I'll shout it." I had him and he knew it. His face turned an ashen hue but I refused to release him.

"Please," he whimpered.

"Whisper it," I hissed violently.

He shot a fearful glance around, then moved his lips against my ear. "Department L," he murmured.

"I know that. What else?"

"I don't know, Joel. Honestly, I don't."

"Did he open the door?"

"Shhhh!"

"Talk," I insisted.

"I don't believe so, not yet."

"Where's he at?"

"I don't know. So help me, that's the truth, Joel. You'll have to believe me." Pale and shaken, he suddenly jerked his arm free and stepped back.

"I'm trying to help him," I murmured.

"Don't do it," he warned. He stepped closer again. "Stay out of it, Joel. Stay out if you want to stay alive!" Before I could answer, he turned and scurried across the lobby. Watching him disappear, I felt a tremor of trepidation. There was no doubt but that he was right; the best thing I could do was to forget that I'd ever heard of Mark Randall. But I couldn't forget; it was much too late for that.

I caught the next nucjet to L.A.

While the nation swept past beneath me, I concocted a plan of action. First I'd warn Ann, if I weren't already too late. Next I'd look up an old man in his nineties named Martin Wister. Beyond that I couldn't plan. Over Nevada we began dropping; moments later Los Angeles swept toward us. When the plane landed, I caught an aircab and tried to relax, but found I couldn't. My muscles were taut and anxious, the tension sang in my mind.

I wondered about Ann—what she was doing and thinking, and whether or not she blamed me for the damning profile on Mark Randall. But that didn't bother me as much as Mark Randall's predicament. Or had Randall already been caught? The question staggered me. All I had to go on was Sinclair's assurance that Randall was running. At that, the race seemed destined to be short. If a man scarcely could buy so much as a pair of shoes without a record of the transaction being sent to central computer, it was virtually impossible to remain long hidden. Mark Randall, knowing that, still had elected to run. Why?

I couldn't answer that, yet was certain that Randall knew exactly what he was doing. He wasn't the kind to fly in the blind. More likely he'd planned for this day long ago. At the least he'd calculated his chances, knew the odds. But could anyone long escape Department L?

That didn't seem likely.

I don't know where they came from, where they picked up my trail, how long they'd been following me. I didn't know a thing until a hand touched my elbow, another hand the other. My scalp prickled. I had the desire to keep

walking without looking to either side, to pretend that I
wasn't suddenly being escorted. I also had the urge to run,
the good sense not to.

My apartment building was just ahead. I decided to pass
the entrance, keep walking, see what happened. What
happened was that a voice in my ear said, "Turn in," when
we reached the building. I turned in.

Although the elevator ride seemed endless, it gave me a
chance to scan my new companions. With my unpleasant
habit of characterizing strangers by their appearance,
probably as an aid to memory, I automatically tabbed
them as Sparrow and Big Bull. And the latter *was* big.
Bulky, with eyes like small chunks of coal, ears pinned
close to a narrow skull, he looked stupid. I dismissed him
with a glance.

Sparrow was a different proposition. Slender, with a
bland face, blue eyes that were surprisingly mild and a
touch of hoarfrost in his well-groomed hair, he was the
archetype of the-man-who-wasn't-there. He seemed to
blend into the side of the elevator cage. Yet instinctively I
knew he was the one to deal with.

"I take it that you want to speak to me," I said. My voice
held a cracked sound that I couldn't control.

"As a matter of fact, we do." Sparrow nodded.

"Fire away."

"Your apartment, Mr. Blake. It's more comfortable."

"Mind telling me who you are?"

Sparrow didn't answer. By the time I reached my door
I was boiling, but not enough to make me reckless. Big Bull
was a powerful deterrent. Inside, I stared at Sparrow. He
flipped open a wallet. An identification card read: Sybert
Ryerson, Bureau of Public Safety. I translated that as
Department L. I wouldn't give him the satisfaction of
knowing that it shook me.

Instead I nodded toward Big Bull. "Who's he?"

"Inspector-agent Quinby." Sparrow answered for him.

"So?"

"Sit down, Mr. Blake." Sparrow gestured toward a
chair as if he owned the apartment. Big Bull made himself

comfortable on the davenport. Sparrow eyed me coolly. "What do you know about Mark Randall?" he asked. His voice was as mild as his eyes.

"I did a profile on him. You can read it in the *Solar Press*." It was an exhibition of bravado I didn't feel.

"I already have." Sparrow's thin face registered regret. "What else do you know about him?"

"Only his general reputation as a scientist."

"Nothing more?"

"Nothing that comes to mind."

"Was your contact with him limited to the interview?"

The question alerted me; it rang of a trap. Sparrow knew very well about our dinner date—probably had every word on tape. I hedged by saying, "We met several times."

"Where?"

"At the symposium." I saw his waiting expression and added, "We had dinner at the Sea Frond, off Malibu."

"Just the two of you?"

"Dr. Willett was with us. She's an astrophysicist on the UCLA faculty." I offered the explanation as if he hadn't known.

"Is she close to Randall?"

"She met him for the first time at the symposium."

"Oh?" He arched his brows.

"They were my guests; I invited them."

"You knew her previous to that time?"

"I've met her a few times," I admitted. I decided to take the initiative and asked, "What's this all about?"

Sparrow raised his head in faint surprise. "Don't you read your own paper, Mr. Blake?"

"I read that Dr. Randall had disappeared, yes."

"That's all you need to know." He smiled disarmingly. Big Bull smirked, which made me boil inside. Although he hadn't as much as opened his mouth, I knew he wasn't along just for the ride. Sparrow was a man I could smash with a swat; Big Bull was there to see that I didn't. The muscle and the brain. Yet either one could be tough, no matter how you cut it.

Fighting to control my anger, I looked at them. There was nothing I could say or do, and they knew it. One didn't talk back to Department L. Oh, I suppose a few people had, but they hadn't remained around very long.

"Any more questions?" I asked finally.

"In time," said Sparrow. He gestured to his companion, rose, and stared down at me. His mild blue eyes suddenly were as opaque as stone. "We'll be in touch with you later," he warned.

"I travel a lot," I snapped.

"I'm certain we can always find you." The words, although pleasantly spoken, held a not-so-veiled threat. Not that they weren't true. The BPS operated with sophisticated electronic devices which could scan, listen, track— monitor their quarry through every sleeping and waking moment. A self-contained pea-sized device, dropped anywhere in a building, would pick up its every whisper, broadcast them to a listening post that might be miles away. There a spectrum analyzer would separate one voice from another. Another sensor could unerringly track a certain invisible chemical which, if dabbed on a man's clothes or car, would make his movements as conspicuous as if he were accompanied by a wailing siren.

I don't pretend to know all the techniques; I doubt that many people do. But I knew that I couldn't run far enough or fast enough to escape the BPS, let alone Department L. Ergo, I'd have to pretend cooperation. The idea was sickening.

At the door Sparrow turned back. "If you get a line on Randall, or if he contacts you. . . ." He paused, his eyes expectant.

I forced a smile. "I'll let you know."

"We can be reached any time of the day or night through the local office," he said. As I watched them leave, my unease flooded back. Sparrow had left his little ploy of forced cooperation until the very end, as if by afterthought. That was a psychological ploy.

But where was Mark Randall? The mystery intrigued me. I quickly dismissed the possibility that he might be hiding at Ann's. Sparrow & Company would have had the place bugged from the first. Yet, by the same logic, they would have had their tracers on him since the symposium, if not before. Despite that, he'd managed to vanish into thin air.

One possibility was that he'd been able to detect their sensors, elude them or, more probably, had employed some means to disrupt their operation. Whatever the case, it was evident that Sparrow knew no more of his whereabouts than did I. That was heartening.

Although I had scant doubt that from here on out I'd be a tracked man, Ann a tracked woman, I had to warn her immediately. I debated the safety of it. Somewhere a tape would record our every word, sensors would follow our every move. We'd be living in a glass world. I couldn't forget that, not even for a moment. Neither could she. That's what I had to impress on her. But the surreptitious rendezvous was out. The safest course was to act above-board—meet her openly. And to Sparrow's eyes, I had to appear to be working in cooperation. That was the stinker.

I didn't bother to peer into the rear-view mirrow as I drove toward her house. I knew that I was followed. Either that or some device had been planted in the car to record my moves and transmit them to a BPS listening post.

A solitary light in the upper story told me she was home. I drove up the steep road to the small flat alongside the house and got out. The wind, cool in my face, brought the distant screech of a gull. Seaward, a fog bank was rolling in. Although I saw no sign of car lights on the winding road below, I felt certain someone was watching. Watching and listening.

I knocked sharply, heard movement inside before the porch light flooded on. I was staring at the small rectangle of one-way glass when the door swung open.

"Joel!" Her cry held both gladness and anxiety.

"I'm back, honey." I boomed the words, gesturing covertly to indicate that someone might be spying on us. Comprehension flooded her face.

"I've been waiting," she exclaimed.

I caught her in my arms and moved my lips to her ear. "We're being monitored," I whispered. "Make it real."

"Joel, Joel," she cried ardently.

"Miss me, honey?"

"Every hour, every minute!"

"I couldn't wait to get back." I caught her again and kissed her, this time with real fervor. Not cricket, perhaps, but I told myself I had to make it real. Laughing, she pulled me inside and closed the door. Instantly the laughter vanished, replaced by a look of grave concern. Her eyes asked a thousand questions. I shook my head warningly.

"How was the trip?" she asked.

"Dull, New York was a bore."

"It's been forever." She made it sound so convincing I found myself wishing she meant it. Not that I was fooling myself; I knew I'd been retired from competition the instant Mark Randall had entered her life. And I knew she knew it, which made it easier for us both. But as the saying goes, hope dies hard. Perhaps that's why I nourished the flickering flame.

She caught my hand and led me toward the stairs. Midway up I remembered the story in the *Solar Press* and pulled her to a halt. "I'm not responsible for that column," I whispered. "They changed it."

"I know," she murmured. She squeezed my hand reassuringly. I put on some music, but not so loud or so raucous as to suggest that we were trying to muffle our words. Sitting on the couch with her head on my shoulder, my arm around her, I found myself wishing that there had never been a Mark Randall—that this was the start, instead of, perhaps, the end of dreams. For a while we listened in silence.

Finally she whispered tensely, "Department L?"

I felt a slight shock that she should even know of the dread BPS section. Very few did outside of high government or those privy to government channels, as were a few members of the *Solar Press*. Mark Randall must have told her. If so, perhaps he'd confided all his plans to her. If

Sparrow suspected that! I shuddered at the possibilities, then saw her waiting expression.

"Yes." I nodded jerkily, felt a tremor run through her body. I hated having had to state it so baldly but there was no other way. Neither did she want anything but the truth. I gave her time to absorb the shock before whispering, "Do you know where he is?"

She shook her head.

"Did he make contact?"

"I . . . don't know."

"Did he tell you anything at all?"

"Only that he'd be gone for a while, that the BPS might be looking for him." Her head came up. "He warned me about Department L."

"Anything else?"

She hesitated briefly. "He promised he'd contact me when it was safe."

"Your phone, mail, everything will be monitored," I cautioned.

"He knows that."

"It won't be for just this month, next month. It'll be for years, if necessary."

"We're prepared, Joel." She asked calmly, "What do you know about him?"

I whispered what little I knew, and what I had surmised. It wasn't much, but the fact that Sparrow & Company were in the dark appeared to assure her.

She turned to face me. "You're taking a terrible chance, Joel."

I wanted to tell her that it was for her, but couldn't. That simply wasn't true. I couldn't deny that she meant the world to me but there was far more to it than that. Had there been no Ann, I still would have jumped to Mark's side. Part of it had to do with the man himself, part with his strange and exciting revelations. And part, I suspect, because he was moving against the establishment. He was declaring his autonomy in a pegboard world, and he was not frightened by Department L. That was the thing, he wasn't frightened—knew nothing of the fear inherent in the rest of us. We had come to accept, but he hadn't. That's what drew me to him. In the end, I said, "All life is chance."

"You have to stay out of it, Joel."

"No, I'm going to find him."

"Don't try it," she exclaimed. "You might lead them to him!"

I shook my head. "He might need help, Ann. I have to try."

"Where would you start?" she asked wonderingly.

"Did you ever hear of Martin Wister?"

"You know?" She stared at me.

"Mark mentioned the name."

"I wouldn't do it," she answered fiercely.

"See Wister, or try to find Mark?"

"Don't do either, Joel. I don't believe Mark would want you to get involved. I'm certain he knows exactly what he's doing. He wouldn't have disappeared without a plan."

"You're worried," I replied pointedly.

"Because of Department L," she confessed. "They're . . . killers!"

"You seem to know a great deal about them."

"Only what Mark told me." Her voice rose above the whisper-stage and I shushed her.

"What are you going to do?" I murmured.

"Wait."

"Nothing more?"

"Not till I hear from him."

"Any idea how long that might be?"

"Days, weeks, years—I don't know." She rose and asked aloud, "Care for some coffee?"

"A cup, strong and black." When she vanished down the stairs, I opened the glass doors and stepped out onto the balcony. The chirrup of crickets filled the air. I wondered how they sounded over electronic pickups.

Off in the west the fog bank had stalled, an imposing gray wall beyond which nothing was visible. It reminded me of what I faced in my quest for Mark Randall. Humanity was the gray pall into which he had vanished. Into which part of the fog should I plunge? The analogy made my task seem hopeless. Yet finding him could be no more miraculous than his disappearance. Flame-haired and six-foot-five or more, he scarcely could hope to blend into the populace.

I speculated over that. If Mark had planned his disappearance ahead of time, as I was certain he had, how might he have done it? The day was far past when a man could simply move to a different part of the world and change his name. In this world of the twenty-third century, every individual who walks the land has an analog that lives in computer center. It is an analog in the form of a name, serial number, vital statistics, credit and tax records, voting registration, education, social-medical records, passport, and a thousand and one things that constantly flow into the government's memory banks. Retrieval of such information was but a matter of moments.

As the system was set up, a person couldn't get a job, obtain credit, secure a passport, or any of a score of other things without being cleared by the computer. But the important thing was that the constantly building record reflected a person's movements. That made it obvious that Mark couldn't hope to escape detection merely by blending into the population.

What did that leave? I didn't know. But I was certain that Mark Randall knew exactly what he was doing. By that reasoning, my best bet was to do nothing, wait until he contacted Ann.

But would she tell me? I could see no reason why she should. There was absolutely nothing I could do to help him. Considered in that light, I wondered at my determination to find him. Was it for Mark Randall's sake, or did it go deeper—some subtle purpose that I had not yet clarified in my mind. I couldn't answer that. But I did know I was committed, that my destiny somehow was linked to his.

As I stood there, the mindlessness of space bearing down on me, I felt utterly insignificant and primitive. A billion ancestral years had gone into my making, yet I was but a transient entity in the maw of time. How could I call my being purposive? And yet, if there was no purpose, why that billion years? Species came and went, but life itself flowed on. That was the thing; there was always life. Still the purpose had to be more than continuity.

The enormity of the night dwarfed me. Like my single-celled ancestors, which once had drifted in the primal seas, I was caught by an immensity too great ever to know. What intellect I possessed made it all the more difficult, for I could grasp the paradoxes but not their answers. Or were such paradoxes answerable? Mark Randall believed they were.

While I gazed at the stars, which lay like white shadows in the black vault above, I reflected on some of the things he'd told me. "Our minds are not primitive; they're merely unused." And another time: "The beginning and the middle and the end are one and the same thing, Joel."

What did he really mean? I couldn't begin to comprehend. That nettled me, for I believed that Ann understood him completely. Or was that due to the silent rivers that flowed between them? Mark spoke of evolution, yet I was certain he hadn't meant evolution in the usual sense. Man, the atom-jiggler, was but little changed from the-man-who-roared-in-the-cave. Less hair, perhaps, but his essential dimensions remained much the same. Or had Mark meant the evolution of the mind? That seemed more logical.

Other universes in the here-and-now! Gazing at the pale, winking lanterns hanging insensate above me, I tried to imagine how that could be. Length, breadth, height—that was the universe I knew, its totality afloat in the intangible dimension of time. Yet Mark held that another universe, perhaps multiple universes, simultaneously existed; or perhaps it was all one universe in which length, breadth, height, and time were but a single dimension. I marveled at that.

Ann's footsteps on the stairs brought me around. She turned down the music and over coffee we chatted, the kind of inconsequential chatter any man might make with a maid. Certainly any listener would find it trivial.

Finally I rose to leave.

"Must you?" she asked wistfully. She had the voice for that kind of acting.

"Work," I answered regretfully. "I'm a slave to the clock."

She laughed. "You should let the clock run down, forget time."

"But time remembers," I answered. "At a certain hour it shouts, 'Joel, where are you?' It's the bloodhound that dogs me." She followed me to the door, turned on the porch light and came outside. Again, for the benefit of possible watchers, she allowed me to kiss her goodnight. If I held her overly long, well, I did have to make it look good.

When finally I stepped back, she said simply, "Good-bye, Joel."

"Good-bye?"

"Goodnight," she corrected. Before I could answer she stepped inside and closed the door. At the bottom of the steep drive I twisted around to look back at the house. At that instant the porch light blinked out.

Like a star being blotted from the heavens.

SIX

The nucjet landed in Chicago several hours before midnight.

The buildings that hemmed the air terminal, rising two hundred or more stories, jutted like spears into the sky. Their lights blended into an avalanche of white flame that gave me a giddy sensation. I averted my eyes as I walked down the ramp.

I had scant doubt that I was under surveillance. The feeling had been with me from the moment I'd met Sparrow and Big Bull. All Sparrow had had to do was ascertain my flight, call ahead, have someone pick up my trail the instant I disembarked. Or my shadow could have flown with me. In either case, I had to shake him (her?) without being too apparent.

With the crowd swirling around me, I glanced about with attempted unconcern. My shadow could be any of the several hundred people still spilling from the nucjet, any of the thousands milling in the terminal. It was conceivable that my movements were being followed on a screen somewhere. Still, I had to take the chance.

Martin Wister, as I'd previously discovered, lived in Winnetka on the shore of Lake Michigan, some miles north of the terminal. Although I knew it was risky, my best chance was to contact him first by phone. After taking what I hoped was evasive action, I slipped into a booth in the noisiest section of the terminal, located his number and placed a call.

I kept my eyes on the instrument's screen. Half a dozen chimes sounded before it flared to life. The face that looked out at me was old and wrinkled, the sparse hair white, but the blue eyes held an alert gleam. I could see him sizing me up. "Dr. Wister?" I asked.

"Speaking." His voice held little of the creakiness of age.

I gave my name and affiliation. "I would like to stop by for a moment if it's not too inconvenient," I explained.

"For what reason?"

"It concerns a mutual friend."

"Who?"

Balanced neatly on the horns of my dilemma, I hesitated. "A friend who has disappeared," I said finally.

His face tilted so that he viewed me down the bridge of his nose. "I have nothing to say to the *Solar Press,* Mr. Blake."

"This is personal," I insisted.

"What is it?"

"I don't like to talk over the phone."

"Well, I'm afraid. . . ."

I saw him preparing to terminate the call and blurted, "I have to know if he made contact!" His gaze changed only slightly, or perhaps I fancied it. His face suddenly seemed to have grown still. The word "contact" must have caught him, told him I could only have gotten it from Mark.

Quietly he said, "Perhaps you'd better stop by." He scrutinized me closely while giving me directions for finding his place. I gave a sigh of relief when the call was terminated. I'd left Los Angeles with a hope and a prayer, but with no assurance whatever that I might contact him. Neither could I have risked calling from the Coast. But as it was, the doors were opening magically. I couldn't ask for more.

I caught an aircab to Winnetka, then a surface cab to the number given me. His home turned out to be an ancient dwelling set on a tree-shaded lot, an anomaly among the spires that soared around it. The grounds must have been worth a fortune. Martin Wister was either very wealthy, very eccentric, or both.

The cab driver pulled up in front. "Shall I wait?" I

shook my head, not wanting to get caught with any commitments. As the cab's lights blended with traffic, I turned to scrutinize the house more closely.

Squatted among the shadows, its railed porch and second-story balcony spoke of far more years than I'd seen. The architecture was from an age long dead. Gray with time, the house was part of the ancient trees that hemmed it in, part of the green lawn that lay like an oasis in the bustling city around it. A single light shone in what I judged would be the front room.

My footsteps sounded hollowly on the plastic tile as I moved toward the porch. How many years had it been since I'd heard my footsteps in a city? I marveled at that, and at the quietness. The doorbell brought the soft tinkle of chimes.

I waited for a moment, then rang again. Remembering that Martin Wister was in his nineties, I feared he might have dozed off. When a knock did no good, I moved to the lighted window and peered in. As I did, I jerked straighter. My hands began to shake. Martin Wister was there, all right. His body sprawled on the floor, his ancient face shone white under the glow of a lamp. It held the serenity of death.

My first thought that he'd suffered a heart attack was violently dismissed. Not that men in their nineties weren't subject to seizures, but I couldn't buy the timing. Department L! The name stabbed at my mind.

I suppressed the instinct to run, get away while I could. If I were under surveillance, flight would be a damning indictment against me. And once I ran, I'd keep running; in time I'd be fleeing my own shadow. I couldn't live with that future. My pride and anger and stubbornness wouldn't allow it.

Despite my determination, I felt the icy touch of fear. It lay in the pit of my stomach and in my mind at the same time. Slowly withdrawing from the window, I gazed into the shadows around me. The night seemed empty of threat.

With my heart thudding in a steady, loud beat, I edged

slowly toward the front door. I don't know whether I was surprised, relieved, or frightened to find it unlocked. I entered cautiously, and stood just inside with my senses attuned. The silence told me nothing.

There was no reason to feel for Martin Wister's pulse. Purplish blood rimming the burned slash of a laser gun above one ear verified what I had instinctively known. It had been death, sudden and silent. And recent!

I straightened slowly, tense and alert, scarcely daring to breathe. The killer could be only moments away, or still in the house. The realization brought beads of perspiration to my brow. One couldn't fight a laser beam. But my scalp didn't prickle; I had no sense of *presence*. The only sense was the sense of death; it was mirrored there in Martin Wister's ancient face. I edged back into the dark entrance hall to give me time to think.

"Perhaps you'd better stop by"—as Martin Wister's last words echoed in my mind, I cursed myself for a fool. I should have known that his phone would be monitored. No matter how I looked at it, my call had been his death sentence.

But why Martin Wister? I felt certain I knew the answer. Wister had known of Mark Randall's research, had consulted with him on it. He'd known why Randall had vanished, why he was being sought. Like me, he'd been kept alive in the hope that Randall might contact him again. But when I'd called, he'd had to be silenced.

I examined the deduction. It appeared obvious that Wister hadn't known Mark Randall's present whereabouts. If he had, the BPS—Department L, I should say—would have tortured it out of him. Big Bull was the man for that. The department's certainty that Wister hadn't known to what destination Mark Randall had fled indicated the degree of surveillance to which he had been subjected. He'd lived under the same glass as I.

The reason that I wasn't lying on the floor alongside him was abundantly clear. Sparrow & Company still hoped that Randall might contact me, or that I might stumble onto some clue to his whereabouts. The Judas goat—that was my value. Although it wasn't flattering, it did provide a certain immunity. I felt I'd need it.

I resisted the impulse to search the house for possible clues that might point up the exact nature of the research Wister and Randall had shared. If any existed, Wister would have hidden them in a place all but impossible to find. And should I find them, I would be a step closer to my death, for my usefulness would be diminished by that much. That last was the most convincing argument of all.

My last sight of Martin Wister was of the ancient face, framed in its sparse white hair, lying in the circle of light cast by the lamp. The blue eyes stared blankly at the ceiling. I wondered to what far horizon he had fled.

With the wind cool in my face, I closed the door behind me and returned along the plastic walk. My nerves twanged with the tension. Several blocks away I located a public phone, called an aircab, and moments later was soaring toward the central air terminal. That gave me time to think.

It would be of no use to attempt to conceal the fact that I'd found Martin Wister murdered; Sparrow & Company knew better. Besides, any attempt to hide it would indicate non-cooperation, which would give them a dim view of my activities. But I would be justified in not reporting it, for that would indicate my knowledge that secrecy was required. That *was* a form of cooperation.

I debated the logic. Regardless of personal considerations, Martin Wister was a famous name; he was news. The least I could do was to tip Harvey Sinclair to what had happened, let him ignore it on his own.

One other thought occured: I had set myself up as a clay pigeon. If Sparrow & Company could prove that I was on the premises, they could pin the murder on me and probably make it stick. I didn't want to think about that. I looked at the sallow quarter moon low in the east; it was near the witching hour.

From Chicago I caught a nucjet to New York. The anti-fogs had cleared the airport so that when we came out of the dense shroud, the terminal below, in its vast circle of light, sparkled as brilliantly as a Nevada city. At three o'clock in the morning it was as busy as at high noon; that was the nature of life there. Afterward, I caught a few hours sleep in an anonymous hotel.

I rose early, bought a morning edition of the *Solar Press,* and popped into a nearby cafe for breakfast. As I spread the paper on the table, Mark Randall's picture leaped to my view. The words under it read: *Famed scientist sought in misappropriation of funds.*

So, Harvey Sinclair had been right—they were trying to pin a juggling act on him. Not that they actually intended to hook him on it; that was merely to destroy his public image. What they intended, I knew, was death. Martin Wister's fate was the precursor of things to come. Or so they planned.

I scanned the story hurriedly. A compilation of generalities, it offered plenty of accusation but little fact. That was standard procedure. Karl Burger, the director of the BPS, stated that an arrest was expected momentarily. That was another stock line. The story was the kind a host of people would be all too ready to believe. For some perverse reason we get a kick out of seeing a big name toppled, just as we secretly applaud the rascal who makes it big. That is one of the ironies of human nature.

No one had to tell me where the story came from; it was a typical BPS handout. It was evident that Harvey Sinclair had used it without a single word-change. I didn't like that, although I knew he had no choice. He was playing the role of middleman.

Aside from that, Mark Randall's private research was of the mind, philosophical in nature rather than the objective approach of the lab. What he termed research was a looking inward; that required genius, not money. It was also the kind of research that few people understood.

A quick scan through the rest of the paper failed to reveal any mention of Martin Wister's murder; or perhaps I should say suicide, for that was certainly the way it would be branded. Unless they decided to pin it on me.

That brought a grimace. Or perhaps they'd say nothing; they'd let the old man go his way unannounced.

I pushed the remainder of my breakfast aside—it was ruined anyway—and caught a cab to the immense pile of rock that housed the *Solar Press*. Sinclair's secretary, a pale blonde with pinpoint eyes that spoke of a drug journey, appeared startled at my entrance.

"Mr. Sinclair's not in," she blurted.

"When do you expect him?" Her disconcerted manner brought a tinge of unease.

"You'd better see Mr. Carmody." Her voice rose almost to a shrill wail.

"Why?"

"Please, Mr. Blake." She wrung her hands helplessly. I stared at her distraught face, then wheeled and marched toward Ed Carmody's office. My thoughts were jumping like grasshoppers. What I knew of Carmody I didn't particularly like. As Harvey Sinclair's second-in-command, he was prone to wield his power a bit too brutally. Nor was he as direct and forthright as Sinclair. But he was a good editor; I couldn't take that from him.

This time I was ushered directly in. Carmody rose to greet me, his long face a study in speculation. He stuck out a hand. "Glad to see you, Joel." The greeting was automatic.

"What's up?" I queried sharply.

"Sinclair was murdered this morning. We just got the report."

"Murdered?" My chest muscles contracted in a sudden spasm.

"That's off-the-record," cautioned Carmody. "Officially it's suicide. He had a laser gun in his hand."

"How do you know it was murder?"

"A man doesn't shoot himself in the back of the head." Carmody's gaze sharpened. "I wouldn't have mentioned it except that the whisper is sweeping the building. You'd have heard it sooner or later."

"Aren't you going to investigate it?"

He shook his head. "The orders are to let it lie."

"Whose orders?"

"From above. Someone on the board doesn't want a scandal in the official family."

"Even if it's murder?"

"Even if it's murder," he agreed.

"You'll buy that?"

"Do I have a choice, Joel?"

I sank slowly into a chair, my eyes fixed on him. I couldn't feel bitter toward him; he was a pawn in a game too big for him. Somehow someone—Department L, I reflected savagely—had caught wind that Sinclair knew more about Mark Randall than he'd let on. That knowledge had brought his death.

The flood of guilt came again. Sinclair's was the second death that could be chalked up to my intervention in the Randall story. Not that I wanted to believe it. After all, Sinclair had had an initial contact—the person who had first tipped him to Mark Randall's activities. But that was a weak straw to grasp. Had I not entered the affair, Harvey Sinclair probably would still be alive.

Aware of Carmody's gaze, I said slowly, "No one who knew Harvey would believe it was suicide."

"I realize that." He nodded.

"Won't it look suspicious if you don't investigate it?"

"That's up to the board, Joel. I'm not calling the shots."

"Any idea why he might have been murdered?"

"None," he answered flatly. I closed my eyes, and took time to collect my thoughts. Ed Carmody, whether he knew it or not, could just as unwittingly be drawn into the Randall case—could wind up a suicide, his brain fried by a laser. As Sinclair's second-in-command, he probably already was under surveillance. At the least he'd be tabbed to carry out the crusade, run the BPS handouts. Although I didn't particularly like him, I had to warn him. I owed the *Solar Press* that much.

"Will you be taking over?" As I asked the question, I scrawled the words *keep talking* on a scrap of paper and extended it for his view.

He glanced at it and said, "I'm not certain. The board of

directors is meeting today. I have an idea that I might be, Joel. Not that I can fill Harvey Sinclair's shoes."

While he continued in that vein, I wrote: *Office bugged. Department L. The Mark Randall case. Steer clear of it. Don't go beyond the BPS handouts.*

Carmody scanned the note. A frown crossed his face, but that was all. I motioned to him to keep talking and wrote: *Scientist Martin Wister murdered in Winnetka last night. I'm going to discuss this as I'm certain Department L knows I was there. It's connected with the Randall case.* As I pushed the note toward him, I prayed I wasn't being viewed on a screen somewhere. He glanced at the message and nodded.

"I ran into a murder last night," I said. "Martin Wister. You might recall the name. Someone used a laser on him."

"Sounds familiar." Carmody spoke as if probing his memory. "Wasn't he quite a name in science a few decades ago?"

"A neurophysiologist," I agreed. "I was going to do a profile on him as part of a Famous Names in Science series that Harvey suggested some time ago. I found him with a trench in his head."

"Any idea why he was killed?" It was a dangerous question, yet one that any listener would expect Carmody to ask. Not to have done so would have been suspicious.

"Probably walked in on a robber," I replied. "He was in his nineties, lived alone on a piece of property worth a fortune. Someone might have thought he had a bundle stashed away."

"Murders happen everyday," observed Carmody. "It's not much of a story."

"A paragraph at best," I agreed. "I didn't bother to get involved."

Carmody flattened the note on his desk and wrote: *How do you know Wister was connected to Randall?*

My thoughts leaped. The true answer was far too dangerous to me. Unhesitantly I wrote: *Harvey tipped me.*

He scribbled: *Did he assign you to push the case?*

I nodded, then wrote: *I've declared myself off of it as of last night.* I forced a smile as I pushed the paper toward him. I hated to blame a dead man, but the dead were beyond suffering.

Carmody read it and said, "I think you're wise." As we discussed my future assignments, I meticulously shredded the note into smaller and smaller bits, chewed it into a gummy ball, and dropped it down a chute into an atomic furnace.

As our conversation began to falter, I rose. "I wish you well with the board of directors," I said. I meant it. As for myself, I wouldn't take the job at triple the salary. The headaches weren't worth it.

"It's a big job," he assented. The awe in his voice wasn't put on. We shook hands and I took my leave. As I passed through the outer office I saw the pale blonde again. Her grief assuaged, she was busy making up her face in a mirror. The sight reminded me that grief, too, was transient. In a few months the name Harvey Sinclair would scarcely be remembered. So what had been purposive about his life? The answer was beyond me.

Outside I looked up through the canyons at a blue ribbon of sky. It reminded me of a river flowing through chalk cliffs. What lay ahead? Perhaps I'd wind up on a cement floor somewhere, my brain fried with a laser beam. *Well known columnist kills self*—I could fairly see the headlines already. The picture wasn't especially cheering.

Aside from that, I held a rage in my heart. I hadn't known Martin Wister, yet I sensed that I had understood him very well. Gentle, brilliant, he'd held a secret hope for mankind. Such men were rare. But Harvey Sinclair's death really hurt. My grief was personal. He had his faults, we all have, but we'd liked and trusted each other completely. Such trust is rarer yet. If he'd been jittery about Department L, at least he'd had the courage to give me the go-ahead.

I owed something to Harvey Sinclair; and when it came to that, also to Mark Randall, to Ann Willett, and to myself. If I let the murders pass, if I let Mark Randall get dragged into the dust without trying to help, I could never hold myself in the same esteem again. That's important if a man is to live with himself.

Yet what could I do? Common sense told me to quit—the game wasn't worth the risk; my rage, and a sense of debt, urged otherwise. Neither could I see a compromise; there were no grays of action.

Gazing up at the towering walls of my canyon, I felt myself to be the most futile of motes. Sparrow & Company didn't bother me half so much as the dimensions of the machine they represented. And its invisibility. Awesome in its power, it permeated practically every facet of human endeavor. Now the machine, in effect, had said: Stop Randall. Who was I to say nay. The contemplation of the machine, its deadliness, made me want to draw back, yet I couldn't withdraw; it was far too late for that. It had become too late the instant I had peered through the window and saw Martin Wister's body on the floor, a laser slash through his head.

But it went even beyond that. It extended back to the time when I'd first sat opposite Mark Randall, had listened to him speak of the future of man, of wondrous vistas that lay beyond our senses. And the door to them was in his mind, my mind, every mind. We had but to find it.

He'd started a flame that night; I'd felt its heat ever since. It was the flame of insatiable curiosity. Part of it had to do with the true nature of time, of space, of life itself—with the magnificent dreams Mark Randall had imparted. But part of it was personal. Was I, Joel Blake, a transient event in the scheme of life, or was I something more? I had to know.

And there was Ann. At the thought of her I could all but hear the plaintive cry of a violin echoing through lonely hills, a violin that whispered strange truths in a language I failed to comprehend. Whatever its message, Mark Randall had understood, yet it was too intangible for even him to put into words. Each man was his own translator—he'd said that once, now I knew what he meant. The real music is in the mind of the listener. Still, I'd like to know what he heard. Looking up into that blue ribbon of sky, I knew one thing: my life would never again be quite the same.

I remained in New York for Harvey Sinclair's funeral. Following the services, his body was transported into orbit, then projected into a trajectory that would end in the blazing furnace of the sun. The latest in cremation, it was also something more—the symbolic expression of seeking the candle which, in the beginning, gave rise to all life.

Like moths, we sought the flame.

SEVEN

I reached Los Angeles early in the afternoon and immediately tried to contact Ann. Her phone had been disconnected. I was stewing about it when a knock came at the door. I was neither surprised that it was Sparrow and Big Bull, nor that they had arrived within a few moments of the time that I had. Why should I be? If the truth were known, I probably was never out of their sight.

"Stopped by to ask if you'd heard anything," Sparrow explained. Big Bull smirked.

"Nothing good." I waited while they made themselves at home on the couch.

Sparrow eyed me interestedly. "Been out of town?"

"Chicago and New York," I admitted. His expression told me that he knew everything about Chicago and New York, merely was waiting to hear what I might say, or not say. "I had a nasty shock back there. Harvey Sinclair—he was my boss—killed himself. Used a laser on the back of his head."

"Why'd he do that?"

"Who knows? Perhaps life got too big."

"That happens, Blake."

"The cure's too drastic for me," I admitted.

"You mentioned Chicago." His gaze sharpened.

"Ran into a murder," I said, "or perhaps it was a suicide. Another laser."

"Oh?"

"A retired scientist named Martin Wister, a fellow in his nineties. I found him with his brain fried."

"What makes you think it was murder?"

"I didn't notice a weapon around, but then I didn't look

too hard. Frankly, I didn't want to get caught in the legalities."

"Why'd you go to see him?"

"On the surface, to do a profile on him for a Famous Names in Science series that Sinclair suggested some time ago. He was a neurophysiologist, quite famous in his day."

"And below the surface?"

"I was hoping to get a line on Mark Randall." I caught the flicker of surprise in his eyes and knew he'd been certain I would lie. I risked a glance at Big Bull. He watched me stonily.

Sparrow asked, "What made you think he might know about Randall?"

"I understand Randall was a protegé of his."

"Who told you that?"

"Harvey Sinclair mentioned it in passing when we first discussed the series."

"Sinclair, eh?" His surprise showed.

"Harvey kept on top of most things," I observed mildly.

"He talked himself to death, Blake."

"What do you mean?"

"Just an observation." He smiled gently. "Some people talk too much, some not enough. Either way can be dangerous."

I caught the message. Sparrow was certain that I knew more than I'd told him, and he was letting me know that he knew it. Nothing is quite so convincing as a threat with teeth in it. I didn't quite know how to reply so I let it pass. Sparrow lifted his gaze slowly, letting it linger on my face. He meant it to be disconcerting, and it was, especially as I was on uncertain ground.

Finally he asked, "What's your real interest in finding Mark Randall?"

"He's news," I objected. "We play him up every day in the *Solar Press*. When a nation's top scientist juggles the books, that's big news."

"Any other reason?"

"Isn't that enough?"

"It's fairly convincing," admitted Sparrow. His smile got a bit frosty. "Any other leads?"

"None." I shook my head. "Looks like the case is closed."

"It's not closed. The BPS never drops a case until it's solved. Not this kind."

"I was talking about my interest."

"That's not closed either," said Sparrow. "Please don't think that it is." He made it sound like a request.

"Well, if I can help. . . ."

"I have every confidence that you can, Blake." He rose and Big Bull struggled to his feet. "Just keep trying."

"If you say." I hated myself for my meekness, yet knew there was no other way to play it. Eventually I might run afoul of Sparrow, but I couldn't afford it yet. I was more use to Ann and Mark Randall alive. And to myself.

Watching them depart, I pondered the conversation. It was obvious that Sparrow believed I was holding something back. He'd also been anything but delicate in suggesting what might happen if I talked too much, or not enough. In effect, I'd been warned to keep my mouth shut to everyone but him. The only trouble was that I had nothing to say, either to him or to anyone else. The sum of my knowledge, with regard to Mark Randall, approximated zero.

When they were gone, my thoughts reverted to Ann. Her disconnected phone had me fretting. While I showered and dressed, I weighed a dozen innocuous reasons to account for it, all of which I realized were rationalizations to still my worries. Bitterly I reflected that I should have asked Sparrow about her. He would know; he knew everything. Not that he would have answered. I hurried down to my car with the feeling that I was on television. Perhaps I was.

When I hit the winding road beyond the university, I rolled back the top and stepped up my speed. There was a savage pleasure in the feel of the power beneath my hands, the sliding of tires on sharp curves, the cold wind whipping my face. If it was dangerous, it was the antidote I needed. I couldn't afford to believe that my world was too secure. That *was* dangerous.

Sight of her house perched in loneliness at the edge of the canyon brought back my trepidations. As I climbed the steep drive I saw that her car was missing. Despite that, I hurried to the door and knocked. When no answer was forthcoming, I stepped back to scan the house. The windows shut, the curtains drawn, it held an aura of lifelessness. She could be on vacation, could have been called away on some emergency. . . . The rationalizations flooded back. Yet intuitively I knew it was something more.

With an uneasy glance at the winding road below, I went around to the rear of the house. Although everything appeared buttoned up tight, the back door had the usual flimsy lock. I'd noticed that before: elaborate safeguards on the front door, almost none on the rear. I'd never understood the psychology of that except that it appears to be universal.

A small tool from the car gained me admission quickly enough. I hesitated in the kitchen while the stillness shouted of emptiness. At times I'd intuitively sensed the presence of people before I either saw or heard them. This time I sensed the absence of life. Not only was it the overwhelming sense of a house deserted, but of a house abandoned.

I gazed slowly around; everything was clean and tidy. Dishes and pots had been put away, the towel rack by the sink was empty. I flipped a switch and found that the electricity had been turned off. That implied planning. Pausing in the front room only long enough to determine that everything was in order, I went upstairs.

The rack of musical instruments, the shelves of books, the locked glass doors to the veranda—everything appeared in order. I was about to leave when suddenly I remembered something. Crossing the room, I jerked open the door of the cabinet next to the rack of musical instruments.

The violin was gone!

I stared at the empty space, my thoughts a tumult. There

was no reason why she shouldn't have taken the violin, of course, but would she take it on a short trip? I don't know why, but something about the missing instrument was like a voice screaming: "I won't be back!"

Deep in my mind I knew one thing: she wouldn't have left unless Mark Randall had contacted her. The corollary of that was that they were in hiding together. Retreating from the house, I locked the door behind me and returned to my car. At the bottom of the drive I looked back. The house had never held such a loneliness as it did at that moment. Would I ever see Ann again? I didn't want to think about that.

I drove to the university and moments later was talking to the dean. He must have anticipated that I was interested in a profile on him for his face was all bland and smiling. The smile turned starchy as I asked about Dr. Willett.

"She requested a year's leave," he answered. "Some kind of emergency." She hadn't left a forwarding address, nor did the school have any record of her family. Later I was to learn that she had none. An only child, both parents were dead. All in all I'd drawn a blank, except for one thing: the leave indicated an intent to return. Either that or she had used it as a gimmick to slide out from under as easily as possible.

When I returned home, I was startled to find Sparrow & Company on the couch. Jolted, I began cooking up answers even before the questions were asked. But Sparrow took his time—the psychological gambit again. And it worked; I felt completely unnerved.

"Where'd she go?" he asked finally. Soft as velvet, his voice held a deadly undercurrent.

"Who?" I tried to appear perplexed.

"This is no time for games, Blake."

"Ann Willett?"

"Who else?"

"I don't know where she is," I protested. "She took a year's leave—an emergency of some sort." I had to say that because Sparrow would get that from the dean soon enough, if he didn't already know.

"Didn't she tell you anything beforehand?"

"Not a word. Something must have happened while I was in the East."

"Who are her closest friends?"

I shook my head. "I don't know. I never heard her mention anyone in particular. She didn't get around much."

"That's not normal," he countered. "All young women get around."

"I still don't know."

"As close as you were to her?"

"I wasn't that close," I answered steadily. Big Bull snickered, an infuriating sound. I fought to keep my temper. The man with the narrow skull was a nobody, a hulking ox with the brains of a gnat. I suppressed the desire to tell him that.

Sparrow watched me, the speculation in his eyes. Abruptly he asked, "Who's Fallon?"

"Fallon?" I don't know why I felt startled, other than that the name somehow must be related to Ann, to Mark Randall. I probed at my memory. "I don't know," I finally admitted.

"You never heard her mention the name?"

"Never." I returned his look coolly. "Why?"

"That's none of your business, Blake."

"I'm looking for leads," I reminded. "How can I help you if you close them off?" It was a logical argument and he knew it. The indecision in his face made me appreciate his predicament. Sparrow was geared to get information, not to give it. He lived in a world of secrecy in which everything flowed in and very little out. That was typical not only of the BPS, and Department L in particular, but of the entire government hierarchy. For some odd reason the citizen was not supposed to know. It was a self-defeating philosophy, yet the men who pursued it seldom appeared to realize it. To that extent I was reminded of Ann's closed loop.

I glanced at Big Bull. His face held a stupid look, as if it were a facade for nothing; I considered that an apt description of his mind. Yet I couldn't allow my prejudice to get the better of me. He was, after all, an agent for Department L, which most certainly represented the super-elite of the BPS. But I still couldn't picture him as anything but a muscle-man—a lummox who barbecued people with lasers at a nod from other people like Sparrow. I made a note to worry about him later.

Abruptly Sparrow said, "I'll tell you as much as you need to know. Fallon called the Willett woman, went through the university switchboard in an attempt to throw us off."

"You couldn't trace the call?"

"We did, but he was gone by the time we got there. So was she. She must have taken flight within minutes."

"When was that?"

"Several days ago."

"From where was the call made?"

"Winnetka." Sparrow's eyes riveted on my face. "Shortly before Martin Wister was murdered."

"My God, do you believe. . . . ?" I stared at him.

"That Fallon murdered Martin Wister? Yes, I believe it."

I started to argue, but stopped, caught with the damning thing which I knew lay in the agent's mind. Preposterous, of course, but it was exactly the kind of thing he would believe. I could see it in his eyes, in the tightness of his lips. I waited for him to put it into words. Finally he did.

"I'm also certain that Fallon is Mark Randall."

"No," I exploded.

"Why not?"

"Randall was Martin Wister's protegé. Why would he murder a man to whom he owed so much?"

"Perhaps to cover his tracks, to keep him from revealing some secret or other. Wouldn't you say that was enough?"

"You wouldn't if you knew Mark Randall."

"You knew him that well?" The question caught me off balance, and for a moment I could only glare at him. His lips curled in secret amusement.

"By reputation," I finally answered. The explanation was weak and we both knew it. In an attempt to cover up, I asked quickly, "What did he say to her?"

"He told her he'd be waiting, that was all. He didn't name a time or place, which tells us their degree of planning." His eyes mocked me. "Looks like your girl friend threw you over."

"Happens all the time. What was Fallon's first name?"

"He didn't give one."

"Sounds like a code name," I suggested. "Chances are the caller won't use it again."

"You believe not?" His expression questioned my judgment. "The caller was Mark Randall; you can accept that as fact. He simply didn't expect the call to be monitored. If he wanted a code name, why Fallon? Smith would be a much more innocuous one. He slipped that time, Blake. For whatever reason, I'm certain that's the name he's parading under."

"He still could change it."

"It's not that easy. It takes time to build a background that can slip past computer center."

"There must be thousands of Fallons," I protested.

"Scores of thousands over the nation," he assented, "but we'll catch him. Whether it's Randall or Fallon or any other name, it'll all be the same in the end."

"I'm certain of that." I hated the agreement bit but I wasn't ready to kick Sparrow in the teeth. When it came to that, I wondered if I ever would be ready. A thought lying at the edge of my mind came to the fore and I asked, "If you knew all this when we talked earlier, why did you let me go out to the empty house?"

"Your reactions were interesting."

"I'm suspect, is that what you're saying."

"Your trip out there proved you didn't know she was gone."

"Certainly I didn't know she was gone," I snapped.

"That's what makes it interesting." He gazed mildly at me. "The picture has changed considerably."

"In what way?"

"Before, we wanted Randall for the misappropriation of

government funds, now we want him for murder."

"I can't believe that he did it!" Despite my better judgment, I had to make the protest.

"Is that because you don't want to believe it?" Sparrow gestured, and for the second time that day I watched the pair trudge from my apartment. When the door closed behind them, I sank wearily into a chair. My mind was in turmoil. That I was still suspect, I had scant doubt. But even that worry was secondary to the one I felt for Mark and Ann.

I tried to fit the pieces together.

Fallon, who could have been Mark Randall, had been in Winnetka shortly before Martin Wister's death. I saw no reason why Sparrow would lie about that. Yet that didn't prove that Fallon had murdered him. Neither did it prove that Fallon was Mark Randall. But I knew that he was. The call to Ann and her immediate disappearance had clinched that in my mind, just as it had in Sparrow's mind.

Sparrow was on the right track, I decided, but he had twisted the facts. Mark Randall, alias Fallon, must have stopped by to bid Martin Wister farewell. Perhaps he'd phoned ahead, just as I had, then had departed from Wister's before the BPS could get there. Or perhaps he'd conducted the entire farewell by phone. In either event, the call would have been enough to sign Martin Wister's death warrant.

The logic brought a glum smile as I recognized it as a device to shift the blame for Martin Wister's death from my shoulders onto Mark Randall's. But it could have happened that way; anything was possible. I held but one certainty: the trigger had been pulled by one of the faceless men who served Department L. And that, perhaps, was the only certainty in Sparrow's mind. Beyond that I couldn't conjecture. All in all it had been quite a day.

But the day hadn't ended yet. I realized that when, in the late evening, I received a call from Ed Carmody. As his face came to life on the screen, I felt tense and edgy.

"Sorry to bother you so soon, Joel." The apologetic beginning wasn't like him.

"Shoot," I said.

"The story we were discussing this morning. . . ." He peered at me down the thin bridge of his nose. The thought that we undoubtedly were being monitored brought a sudden fright. It must have shown on my face for he said quickly, "The Famous Names in Science series."

"Of course." I breathed easier.

"I've been thinking it over. I believe you should pursue it."

"The market for that kind of thing is risky," I answered carefully.

"I realize that, Joel." He hesitated. "But Harvey wanted it that way. I believe we owe him that much."

"I'm not so certain I can get the high-powered names lined up. Some of those birds are difficult to pin down."

"There's no rush. You might sandwich it in as you find time."

"If you believe I should." I don't know why I felt reluctant. I'd been glad for the opportunity when Harvey Sinclair had given me the go-ahead, but Carmody had put it more in the nature of an order. Not in so many words, perhaps, but the pressure was there.

"Incidentally, I got the nod from the board," said Carmody.

"Congratulations, Ed."

"It's going to be tough to fill Harvey's shoes."

"You can do it," I encouraged.

"I'll need plenty of cooperation."

"I'm certain you'll have it."

"You give me confidence, Joel. Incidentally, let me know immediately if you run across any really outstanding name."

I gulped, thinking that a listener would have to be a fool not to catch his meaning. Carmody could wind up baking in the sun; we both could. I promised that I would to keep him from pursuing the subject. After a few more remarks, he terminated the call and the screen went blank.

I sat for a while without moving, my thoughts uneasy. Why, suddenly, had he decided that I should pursue the

Randall story? The question plagued me. Because Harvey
Sinclair would have wanted it that way was pure bunk.
The business wasn't that sentimental.

The bigger question was why Carmody had so willingly
put his neck into a noose. Could he be acting on orders
from Department L? That would make sense. In that event
it would be my neck in the noose, not his.

But I couldn't say I was unhappy. Deep in my mind I
knew I'd pursue the case regardless of what Ed Carmody
or anyone else might have to say. And it wasn't strictly for
Mark Randall, or even Ann.

It was for me.

Half a dozen times in the year that followed I returned
to the house that perched like a bird at the edge of the
cliff. Each time I found it as before—lonely, deserted,
caught in an aura of lifelessness, as if it were set on
verboten ground. Perhaps it was.

I don't know why I kept returning except that I nourished a secret hope, a hope that each time dwindled. The
silence there lay like a blight on my soul.

During that year I saw no sign of Sparrow or his
bullish companion, yet sensed that they were never far
away. Even while traveling around the world the consciousness of surveillance dogged my steps. I couldn't shake it.

For a while, caught in a sea of premonition, I anxiously
followed every news broadcast, fully expecting to hear the
dread words: *Famed scientist kills self!* Vivid nightmares
in which I saw Mark Randall's laser-burned body
sprawled on a floor brought me awake, shouting incoher-
ently, my body drenched with sweat. Or Sparrow's mild
blue eyes would peer at me from under the hoarfrost on
his brows and hair. Somehow that was more fearful yet.

I believed it odd that my terrifying dreams should in-
volve him rather than his brutish partner. Perhaps that
was because I considered Big Bull as pure muscle, a man
who could act only under orders. But Sparrow was the
brain. He could foresee, reason, plan. A brain is a thousand times more potent than muscle.

In time the dreams passed.

Gradually I fell back into my old way of life. New Zealand, Borneo, China, Siberia—the lands whirled underfoot as I pursued my restless way. A second year passed, and a third. Occasionally I wondered where Mark and Ann might be; occasionally I drank a silent toast to them; occasionally at night I fancied I heard, borne in on the wind, the plaintive wail of a violin.

Oddly enough, I missed the visits of Sparrow & Company. It had given me a certain sense of security to see them, know where they were. As invisible men, they were far more threatening. It was the old dictum of the unknown more terrifying than the known. Men usually can face what they can see.

But one morning I awoke with a new sense of freedom. The oppression under which I'd labored was gone. Instinctively I knew that my watchers had withdrawn. The faceless men who had monitored my every move, who had recorded my every word, suddenly were no more. *Why?*

The fear flooding back, I sprang for the visaphone and dialed for a recapitulation of the headline news. *Giant asteroid moved safely into Earth orbit. Seventy die in collapse of sea dome. Huge quakes rock. . . .* When the recap ended with no mention of Mark Randall, I gave a sigh of relief. Had anything happened, he would have made the news. I felt certain of that. The BPS would have pushed the story if only to prove that it didn't pay to juggle government funds.

But I knew the search hadn't ended. The BPS would push it silently, unobtrusively, for decades if necessary. I'd heard of agents who had spent their entire careers in the attempt to solve a single case. Almost always they were crimes against government. Regardless of where Mark Randall and Ann might flee, they could be certain of a Sparrow on their trail. Unless, of course, they had found the door to their greater universe.

I couldn't discount that possibility.

Apparently I had been absolved from further suspicion. I pondered that. It could mean that Sparrow had con-

cluded that I was a dead end—that any connection I might
have had either with Mark Randall or Ann Willett finally
and irrevocably had been sundered. Or it could be a
maneuver to lure me into a false sense of security in which
I might make a brash move. That would imply Sparrow's
awareness that I had known of my surveillance, and would
know of its removal. While complicated, the logic couldn't
be rejected. Still another possibility was that the search
had narrowed to a one-by-one check-off of all the Fallons
of the world.

Shortly afterward, while making a routine visit to New
York, Ed Carmody asked, "Still keeping a sharp eye for
Mark Randall?" Although the question had been casually
put, I tensed instantly.

"He's vanished into the blue," I said.

"How about the girl?"

"I check her house occasionally."

"I can't believe that they won't be caught, Joel."

"Why not?"

"They can't get by without feeding some sort of record
into the computer net. One of these days it's going to
return an error call. When it does, they'll nab them."

"Is that what they're doing, concentrating on the computer?"

"I wouldn't know." He smiled stiffly.

I glanced away, my chest tightening. Just the fact that he
had introduced the subject struck me as ominous. Did
Mark realize the relentlessness of Department L, or would
he lower his guard, secure in the belief that time had
shaken the bloodhounds from his trail? I returned my gaze
to him, trying to discern what was in his mind. His face
told me nothing.

I left his office in a quandary. If it were humanly possible, Mark should be warned that the search was as hot as
ever. Yet I really didn't want to renew the search, in view
of all that had happened. Why should I keep sticking my
neck out? The coward and the hero tussled inside me; this
time it was a draw. But a six-and-a-half-foot flame-haired

giant—how could such a man vanish? That was the most baffling of all.

In the months that followed, Mark Randall was seldom far from my mind. Not that I'd made any overt moves to find him—I told myself the world was simply too big, too crowded, my own resources too meager. If Department L couldn't find him, how could I? Yet I did watch, did listen.

Unexpectedly, the break came in London.

While having a drink at the Explorers Club, where I'd gone as the guest of a local publisher, someone mentioned the name Fallon. I swung around. A gaunt man with the face the color and texture of old leather was conversing with a companion at the bar.

"Fallon?" I interrupted. I was too startled to be polite. He glanced my way.

"A miner on the moon," he explained. "You've been there?"

"Not recently. What was he like?"

"A strapping fellow, six and a half feet, at least. He was working in the diggings at Crater Arzachel. That's east of Mare Nubium, the Sea of Clouds," he explained.

A miner! Gazing at him, I struggled with my thoughts. "What do you know about him?"

"Not much. I was telling my friend how he shoved a giant rock from the tracks just as the ore cars were rushing down. Nick of time, too. The gravity's weaker there, of course—only one-sixth that of Earth—but still it was a superhuman feat. I was with Baker Mining at the time, the headquarters in the Sinus Medii. He. . . ."

"Did he have red hair?" I cut in.

"Red? I can't rightly say." He stroked his jaw. "Even in the air-safe domes and shafts they wear pressure gear in case of a blowout. While working, they decompress, open the faceplates. But perhaps you've seen all that?" He eyed me dubiously.

"I've never been to the mines," I confessed. "Was he married?"

"Well, now. . . ."

"I have a friend named Fallon who disappeared several years ago," I hurriedly explained. "He was big, about the size you mentioned, flame-haired. His wife's name was Ann."

"I wouldn't know." He shook his head. "Those mine settlements are a world of their own. Frankly, I never went near the living quarters, but I've heard plenty about them. The stories would rattle your teeth."

"Did you talk with him at all?"

"No reason to. As I mentioned, I worked at the company headquarters in the Sinus Medii, only occasionally went into the field to check tooling requirements. My visits were with supervision. But I can tell you this: only the dregs hit the lunar mines." He peered at me. "Have you heard of the mines in Oceanus Procellarum?"

I suppressed a shudder. I'd heard of them, all right. Located on the bleak Ocean of Storms, in that awful desolation that lay toward the western limb of the moon's visible face, they were subjects of horror and awe. Only the worst of men and the most embittered resorted to the company blandishments and signed on; few, if any, ever returned. I could but guess at the kind of hell man had created in that terrible place. My face must have reflected my thoughts for he nodded and continued, "Arzachel isn't quite that bad, but it's bad enough."

"He was. . . ." I started to speak, but halted. I'd learn no more. Instead I thanked him and turned away. Mark Randall, a miner on the moon! I could visualize the bleak walls of Crater Arzachel rising eerily into a black and empty sky. I shuddered at what the settlement must be like. Good God, what of Ann?

It was crazy, yet it wasn't so crazy at all. A mining colony on the moon was about the last place anyone would think to look for Mark Randall. Even the computer net couldn't touch him there. Arzachel, a far and lonely place in the sky. But it wasn't too far for me.

Two hours later I was on a nucjet headed for New York.

EIGHT

I've never really minded space travel.

Aside from the discomforts of close quarters and the awkwardness of weightlessness, I enjoy the peace and solitude—the sense of getting-away-from-it-all. The stars, even through leaded ports, are a glory to behold.

To eliminate the necessity of the huge engines that would be required to drive the big freighters upward through that first critical hundred or so miles, where gravity is at its greatest, the ships are assembled in orbit from packaged subsystems and systems hurled upward from the earth. Such ships never touch a planetary surface, but operate orbit-to-orbit. Small ferry tugs do the rest. That still leaves the harrowing problem of getting into orbit.

I hated it.

The particular shuttle plane I'd scrounged, through the weight of my press affiliation, was a ten-place job with a needle-shaped fuselage and wide, variable-sweep wings. Designed for passenger and light cargo service, it appeared almost fragile.

I was thinking of that as the jet scream rose to a high wail and the runway began receding faster and faster under the plane's nose. It was a moment I always sweated out. Then the runway was gone, the sprawl of Nevada cities swept past below. As we accelerated and drove skyward, the wings slowly began to fold back. By the time we reached the stratosphere the plane resembled an arrow.

The engines in the thinning air had a whispery, feathery sound. The sky commenced to darken, taking on a velvet sheen. It held the moon in one arm, the sun in the other. Far below, a line of thunderheads blanketed the west. They appeared like misshapen mushrooms.

The whispery sound of the turbo jets faded away, followed by a brief silence before the ramjets exploded to life. The plane shuddered and leaped forward. I shuddered with it, although the other passengers didn't appear to mind. Most of them struck me as space types.

At around Mach nine or ten a momentary bucking came as the pilot opened the airscoops. As the thin air was sucked into the plane's belly and compacted, the oxygen molecules were stripped away, liquified, and stored for use as an oxidizer for the liquid hydrogen rockets that would drive us through our final leg into orbit.

I peered ahead. At around Mach fifteen the feathery sound of the ramjets died, leaving the absolute silence I always associated with space. It was a silence that made me realize how noisy the world was—even the remote fastnesses of the desert at dusk. There, at least, small creatures rustled in the sage.

Eastward, the sun was an intolerably bright disc, rayless against a nigrescent night that as yet was devoid of stars. The unimaginable emptiness made the eyes ache. I looked down again; the earth was far away.

My seat companion, his eyes closed, began to snore softly. I don't know why it irritated me except that it contrasted sharply with my own uneasiness. Looking at his rough clothes and whiskered face, I consoled myself with thoughts of how he would appear at an executive cocktail party.

The cabin speaker crackled to life.

"Ten seconds to rockets on," a voice blared. With the ramjets shut down, the plane glided in ballistic flight. A low whine filled the cabin as pumps brought the liquid hydrogen and liquid oxygen together in the burn chambers. I braced myself for the shock.

The reaction was instantaneous as the fuel ignited; the plane shot forward with a force that flattened me against the seat. Momentarily dizzy, I blinked my eyes to bring them into focus. I felt like I was riding a Roman candle. The g-forces on my body shifted as the plane, now on automatic, hurtled toward orbital space along a programmed course.

The first sight of the freighter was an awesome one. Appearing like a huge splotched whale, it swam toward us through the darkness. That was an illusion, of course, for we were the pursuers. The pilot had taken over again, and now was going through the intricate maneuvers to achieve rendezvous.

Although the freighter was ugly and scarred by radiation, I was glad to pass through the lock and get aboard. Despite the weightlessness, it held a feeling of solidity, which was more than I could say for the shuttle.

The short hop to the moon—sixty-eight hours, to be exact—gave me ample time to think. Ed Carmody had opposed the trip at first; he couldn't see anything newsworthy in it. I persisted until finally he caved in; then all of a sudden he was enthusiastic. Thinking of it now, I wondered if he suspected my true purpose. The possibility made me sweat. I worried about it for the remainder of the trip.

The freighter bucked and vibrated in retrofire as it slid toward an orbit over the eastern limb of the moon. The surface below was pocked and distorted, a harsh blaze of blacks and whites. The almost circular eye of Mare Crisium stared up at me like a foreboding eye. Twisted mountains crawled over the lifeless crust, rimmed its barren and clefted never-never seas. Shadows of awesome cones cut black shadows in funereal plains.

We made orbit above a ragged arm of the Sea of Tranquility and plunged westward above the equator toward the Sinus Medii, which lay at the exact center of the moon's visible face. The Medii also contained the moon's largest community, mostly housed in vast caverns and tunnels carved from solid rock by atomic fire.

It was difficult to conceive that the stark land whirling past was, in reality, but the Earth's backyard; the frontiers now lay far beyond Mars—on the frozen satellites of Jupiter and Saturn. But the moon was primitive enough for me. The scene was eerie.

The huge crater Copernicus slid past on our right and vast Oceanus Procellarum, the Ocean of Storms, wheeled toward us. I had the impression of a tremendous plain broken here and there by rills, scattered craters, and distorted mountains. Flat and gridded, the bottomland was reminiscent of dry lake-beds baked under a desert sun. It was awesome to realize that the day temperature of 250° F. plunged almost instantly to minus nearly that same figure with the onset of night; or when a man walked from sunlight into a shadow.

The Terminator, the line that separates night from day, rushed toward us. Cutting a jagged sawtooth across mountains and plains, it left the moon's dark quarter splotched and leprous in the earthshine. This latter was the Ghost Moon, a world of half-light in which great upthrusts of primeval rock showed as black velvet blobs against a cream-colored background.

While crossing the moon's hidden face, the captain—or was it the navigator?—arranged for rendezvous with the freight shuttles. I didn't see them rise. They came, two orbits later, like a dozen awkward bugs, multi-legged and with swollen metallic bellies, swarming toward us through the lunar night. Their red and green running lights formed a parade against the stars.

One by one they coupled with the freighter while the cargo was transferred. The process filled the old ship with creaks and bangings that made me hold my breath. The trip down, as usual, was sheer terror, although the crew didn't appear to mind it in the least.

But one thing was favorable: there was no weather. There was only the shuttle's inertial force, the moon's weak gravity, the countering power of the vehicle's retro-thrust—all absolutely predictable forces, so they told me. But my newsman's mind had logged a dozen reports of shuttles that had crashed—certain death for all aboard. The scarred face of the moon, like the shoals of old that had snagged the ships of unwary mariners, here and there held the bleached bones of such tragedies. The knowledge wasn't reassuring.

Under the hellish retrofire, the vehicle bucked and shook as it decelerated to begin its downward flight. At engine shutoff, the silence returned; we went into the long drop. It was the eerie sensation of having leaped into a black elevator shaft.

The circular eye of Mare Crisium whirled past again, followed by the Marsh of Sleep, the flat bed of the Sea of Tranquility. With the central highlands speeding toward us, the rockets blasted to life.

As the shuttle slanted downward under retrofire, the distant domes of the Sinus Medii wheeled toward us. They appeared like small silver blobs against the grayish mantle. Radio and radar towers jutted upward from a nearby ridge. Monorails, like silver cords, radiated outward. One twisted southward in the direction of Crater Arzachel; another plunged across the desert to the west, where lay the dread Ocean of Storms.

Suddenly the ground was rushing upward. A number of huge doughnut-wheeled cargo vehicles rolled out from a lock, moving toward the landing pad with a ponderous, elephantine grace. The shuttle paused, balanced on its needle of retrofire, then began its fiery descent.

The last few seconds were interminable.

The Sinus Medii had a hotel of sorts. Located in a tunnel off the mammoth man-made cavern, which served as a central depot, it was little more than a series of plastic cubes strung out along both walls. A sign at the tunnel mouth announced it as the TRAVELERS LODGE.

The cube assigned to me held a narrow cot that folded against the wall, a scarred desk, a single chair. The lighting was by fluorescent gas; bath facilities were communal. It wasn't luxury but it was sufficient.

Refreshed, I returned to the central depot. The interior was filled with muted sounds that echoed and reechoed until they filled the air with a steady whisper. I was reminded of the rustle of leaves in an autumn wind.

I walked carefully until I'd mastered the light gravity, then moved with more confidence. Despite everything, I felt exhilarated. Even though life on the moon was restricted to relatively small air-safe areas, it held a sense of freedom seldom felt on Earth. Perhaps it was because the moon was still a planet of pioneers, where each man was judged on his individual worth. Locating the monorail terminus, I arranged passage to Arzachel, then returned to my room for a much-needed nap.

Ten hours later, seated in a squat gondola, which was suspended from an overhead rail, I passed through an airlock, shot through a long upward-slanting tunnel and out onto the bleak face of the moon. The gondola appeared as nothing but a long rectangular box. It was difficult for an earthling to realize that on an airless planet where aerodynamic considerations were of no import, and where there was a relatively negligible gravity, the geometry of construction could be focused almost exclusively on the vehicle's purpose. Functional was the word.

Aside from the hunched figure of the operator, I rode alone on a plastic bench. The remainder of the car was filled with containers carrying, I imagine, essentials to life and work in the bleak mining community.

The gondola twisted across a ridge to Crater Mosting, shot above its scarred floor, and passed through a winding gorge to Crater Ptolemaeus. The jagged peaks above me clutched frantically at the sky. Another ridge, then the car sped out onto an arm of Mare Nubium and headed toward the Great Straight Wall, one of the moon's anomalies that scientists still are trying to explain.

I watched the moonscape flash past to keep from thinking. Normally optimistic, I'm apt to discount the negative. But not this trip. No matter how I viewed it, I had the feeling of an impending disaster. In my mind the moon had become Mark's cul-de-sac.

My concern wasn't for Mark alone, for I felt certain Ann was with him. Given another chance, would she repeat her decision? I sensed that she would; the dream—if not Mark—was that compelling. I could understand that. Dreams, wonder, the insatiable curiosity to know—those are magnets that pull man hither and yon, chart his course, often against his will.

I couldn't believe Mark would have allowed her to accompany him unless he had been certain he could protect her. Yet how could one hope to escape Department L? Ultimately, however long it took, they would be found. That seemed equally certain.

The gondola swept into the east and entered a winding gorge. The monorail dipped, twisted, and climbed through a bizarre forest of rock that lay naked and raw under the lunar skies. It was a scene that had changed but little since the beginning of time.

Suddenly the car topped out; spread before me was the vast, saucerlike depression of Crater Arzachel. Ludicrously, there was a sign announcing: BAKER MINING COMPANY. With no eye to see, except for an occasional glimpse from a speeding gondola, it looked out from the very peak of the ridge. To me it exemplified not man's urge to advertise, but to cry out to the universe who and what he was.

The wild desolation was appalling. Gazing at the wild tangle of rock and the death-gray plain below, I shuddered at the kind of life Ann must be leading. Could she possibly be happy? The question was laden with poignancy.

Rock and sky abruptly were blotted out as the gondola plunged into a downward-slanting tunnel; simultaneously it began to decelerate. Red lights blinked in the darkness ahead. Moments later it came to a halt, waited while the big doors of an airlock slid open, then crept forward.

"End of the line," the gondola operator bawled. It was the first time he'd spoken.

The superintendent of Baker Mining was beefy, with shaggy brown hair, curious eyes, and the leathery skin of a spacer. He nodded approvingly as I explained that I was doing a story on the Solar Dynamics Corporation, of which Baker Mining was a subsidiary. His reaction was strictly red carpet.

He boomed cordially, "My services are at your disposal, Mr. Blake. However I can help." He gestured expansively. Obviously relishing the prospect of publicity, he launched into a brief history of the company, its products, its expansion rate. I taped the information for effect. From what he said, I wondered why anyone would ever want to work anywhere other than in Crater Arzachel.

During a pause, I said, "By the way, I understand you have a man by the name of Fallon working here."

"Fallon?" He wrinkled his brow.

"He was once a professional strong man," I explained. "A huge fellow, about six-and-a-half feet."

"Oh, that one." Comprehension flooded his face. "That's Big Red. What about him?" He peered quizzically at me.

"I thought it might make a good kickoff for the article —world's strongest man now has moon's toughest job, something like that."

"Clever." He nodded. "There's only one trouble; he's no longer with us."

"Oh?" I felt a stillness inside me.

"He signed up for the Procellarum mines."

"Procellarum?" I was thunderstruck. "Why?"

"Who knows?" He shrugged. "We have a good operation here—excellent working and living conditions. Our fringe benefits are tops."

"There must have been a reason," I persisted.

"It's not unusual for men to court their own destruction, Mr. Blake. I've seen lots of that in my time."

"When did he leave?"

"Several days ago." His tone dismissed the whole thing as trivial. It made me wonder how many men he'd seen leave this hell-hole for one far worse.

"What of his wife?" I asked edgily.

"Wife?" He arched his brows, then crossed the room and consulted a small index file. My heart thumped as I waited. Finally he turned back. "He does have a wife. That's quite unusual. Most men who come here are loners."

"Did she leave with him?"

"Undoubtedly. They're probably still at the central depot."

"The Sinus Medii?"

"He has to go through the processing center there." He smiled cynically. "The law requires a physical examination, record clearance, things like that."

The rest of our conversation was meaningless. Finally I went through the motions of allowing a guide to escort me down into the black tunnels and caverns where men, like moles, burrowed ever deeper into the ore-rich depths. I wouldn't have bothered except that I had to wait for return transportation.

Despite my guide's assurance that the mines were air-safe, I kept one hand near my faceplate, prepared to close it instantly. I'd heard too much of sudden lock failures in which entire shafts and domes suddenly had been depleted of air. Death, on the moon, was a constant visitor.

The cumbersome figures working in the neon glare, their shadows cast grotesquely on the walls, reminded me of a scene from Dante's *Inferno*. I could picture Mark Randall working there, his gigantic body hunched against one of the huge drills that bit into the dark rock. The setting was cast for him.

The guide explained that metal wasn't common on the moon, but where it exists, it exists in plenty. Neither was it native to the moon. Instead, it had arrived in the form of huge meteorites which, in the dawn of time, had crashed through the surface mantle. Great masses of such metal exist in places like Crater Arzachel, and in the farthest reaches of the Ocean of Storms.

I was glad to return to the surface—look up into the black pit of the sky and see the Earth, a golden apple in quarter-light. I thanked the superintendent—MacAbbey was his name—and rode the gondola back through the bleak gardens of the moon.

As the silver vehicle—silver to reflect the awesome heat of the day—zipped between winding gorges and across crater floors toward the Sinus Medii, I tried to untangle my thinking. Mark Randall's abrupt departure from the mines of Crater Arzachel had occurred about the time I was frantically preparing to leave Earth. The timing was too coincidental to be happenstance. It was almost as if he were fleeing from me.

Suddenly I sat straighter. *Fleeing* was the key word. Certainly he wouldn't have left Arzachel for a far worse life unless he'd sensed the approach of danger. But he wouldn't have reacted that way to me; ergo, he was fleeing from someone else!

Sparrow! I recoiled as the agent's thin face with its mild blue eyes flared to life in my mind. Sparrow had discovered that Mark Randall was on the moon! The certainty gripped me. But how could he have known? Several possibilities struck me.

One was that I'd been under surveillance, that my conversation with Ed Carmody had been taped. Sparrow might have deduced, from my insistence on the trip, the reason for it. Almost as quickly as the thought occurred, I dismissed it. There had been no surveillance; I was positive of that. Surveillance can be *felt,* or at least I had felt it. It had been like a physical touch. That feeling had been gone for a long time.

Another possibility was that Ed Carmody had guessed my reason for the trip, had inadvertently revealed it or, worse, had sold out to the BPS. Startling as the latter was, it lay well within the realm of reason. The BPS had tentacles that extended into almost every facet of human life. No one man really knew the ten thousand faces under which it paraded. Except, of course, Karl Burger. The BPS director was the master policeman of all time.

Still, neither of those surmises explained how Mark Randall had learned of his danger. That question was most tantalizing of all. If Ed Carmody had guessed the real reason for my trip, had he warned Randall? That would imply Carmody's suspicion that I had thrown in my lot with the BPS. Ridiculous, of course, yet in Carmody's eyes it might make sense. But why would Carmody risk his neck to warn Randall? Although that made less sense yet, I couldn't discount it. The warp and woof of human contact and purpose was far too involved for that. In the end, I had no answer.

When the gondola pulled into the Sinus Medii, I went directly to a public phone and called the superintendent of Baker Mining. He blinked when he saw my face on the screen. I asked, "Do the men in the mines have ready contact with the outside?"

"Contact?"

"By phone or message."

"By message, certainly. We're not that uncivilized, Mr. Blake."

"Would you know if Fallon received any recently?"

His face froze. "I'm certain I wouldn't. We don't record mail." He'd realized, finally, that I had no intention of doing a story on Baker Mining, that the whole thing had been a blind. His expression said that he didn't appreciate being played for a sucker. I couldn't blame him for that.

As the screen went blank I felt a sense of urgency. Whatever I did had to be done quickly. Yet what could I say when I found them? It was evident that Mark already knew of his danger; his flight from Arzachel gave certainty to that. I couldn't even suggest a place to hide, for there was no place to hide. Not on the moon. Not even in the desolate Ocean of Storms. That seemed the final trap.

But I had to find them. Endeavor in the face of futility is better than no endeavor at all. Translated, that meant that I had to act to keep from thinking.

The tunnel which housed the men awaiting processing and transportation to the mines of Oceanus Procellarum was primitive beyond belief. Bored with the controlled flame of an atomic disintegrator, it was scarcely more than a glorified mine shaft. The small plastic cabins that lined the walls were scarred and unkempt. The ground underfoot had been reduced to dust by the passage of thousands of feet.

I peered at the occasional dwellings that still displayed numbers, searching for the one that the clerk at headquarters had given me. As I penetrated farther and farther into the gloomy shaft, I sensed a growing claustrophobia. The dim lamps spaced along the curving walls did little to dispel the blackness.

Despite an occasional hum that told of an airfan, the atmosphere was stale, fetid, unmoving. It hung heavy in my lungs. My garments soon were soaked with perspiration. I wondered how men could live under such conditions and keep their sanity.

Now and then I glimpsed small groups of men conversing in the shadows. Their voices echoed off the walls in eerie whispers. What could men talk about who were going to certain death? Perhaps they welcomed it, or didn't care. But the question intrigued me. The science that had captured the planets and satellites had not as yet pierced the veil of motivation, let alone the deep wellsprings from which it arises.

A few men sat alone. Under the glare of the lamps, they gazed into the emptiness, their faces vacuous. Seemingly they were unaware of my passage. I was reminded of the ancient catacombs. This was like that: a place of the dead. If the bodies still lived, the rest was gone.

Sight of the living dead around me recalled the superintendent's remark that it wasn't unusual for men to court their own destruction. I thought that it was true—that men court it in many ways. To some it is a game, to some a challenge, to some an end in itself. But of all places to die, none could be worse than this.

All at once from far ahead, haunting and sad, came the sound of music. I stiffened, peering into the gloom, then I recognized it—the lonely cry of a violin.

I stood motionless, waiting, thinking that my mind was playing me tricks. It came again, low and unbelievably poignant, a melody that whispered of things that I could but imagine.

Caught with a fierce exultation, I plunged deeper into the tunnel.

NINE

My knock brought the music to an abrupt halt. The moment was heavy with silence before I heard quick movement inside. An instant later the door was flung open. Limned against the lamplight, Mark Randall's gigantic figure filled the entrance. His clothes, soiled and worn, gave him an unkempt appearance.

"Joel," he bellowed. A pleased smile wreathed his face. Over his shoulder I glimpsed Ann's startled expression. Mark grasped my hand, pulled me inside and slammed the door. Still clasping her violin, Ann sprang forward with a glad cry. I caught her, kissed her ardently, lifted her and kissed her again before setting her down.

"Joel, Joel," she exclaimed. Her eyes glistened.

"You look wonderful," I breathed. Despite the hard life at Arzachel, she really did. Her face reflected a radiance and freshness that was startling. Her eyes fairly sparkled.

"How did you find us?" asked Mark. His gaze grew intent. I told him about the chance remark in the Explorers Club that had sent me winging outward from Earth.

"I had to know," I explained.

"We're so glad you came," cried Ann. "We've thought of you a lot. Tell us about yourself."

"A device to keep me from asking questions," I accused.

"We're here, Joel. That's all that matters."

"Here and running."

"Please," she whispered.

"We have to talk about it," I argued.

"Yes, we're running," interrupted Mark. "There's no reason for not admitting it. But first tell us about yourself."

I began to speak, omitting nothing. A look of pain

crossed his face when I described how Martin Wister had been struck down by a laser beam. "The BPS has accused you of that," I added.

"I would expect that." He nodded soberly. "They could be right, Joel. He might be alive today if I hadn't called to bid him good-bye."

"Not a chance." I shook my head. "They had him under the glass. They let him live only as long as he was useful as bait."

"But a man in his nineties," protested Ann. Her face held disbelief.

"What has age to do with it?" I demanded. "They will kill anyone they believe dangerous to them."

"You're right," agreed Mark.

"If there's any guilt, I share it," I admitted. "I phoned him shortly before he was murdered." I told them about Harvey Sinclair's death, the visits of Sparrow and Big Bull, the abrupt removal of the surveillance that had dogged me for months. They listened quietly until I had finished.

"It's such a waste," cried Ann. "Martin Wister, your Harvey Sinclair; where will it end?"

"I'm more interested in your present predicament," I countered. I looked at Mark. "I'm certain the Department L agents know you're on the moon. I don't know how they found out, but they did."

"How do you know that, Joel?"

"Because you know it. You're running. I didn't know it when I left Earth, but I know it now. I know it and I'm scared."

Mark said quietly, "We've been expecting it."

"How did you discover they knew where you were?"

"We were warned."

"Yes, but by whom?"

"I can't answer that, Joel."

"No, you can't," I agreed. "The question wasn't tactful."

"We have friends, a few." The ghost of a smile touched his lips. "I can't risk placing them in jeopardy."

"I can appreciate that." I studied him frankly. "But I'm

curious, that's my nature. The questions keep pounding at my mind."

Mark raised his eyes. "What specifically?"

"I can't answer that. I really don't know. Some of it has to do with the things you've told me, some with the reason for Department L's frantic search to find you. That last makes me realize how big the stakes must be. But what are the stakes? I sense them but vaguely, just enough to tantalize my mind. Yet it's more than that. Dream and reality —if I can use that term—seem hopelessly intermingled, as if a lot that is happening is happening in a shadow world. My thoughts are formless, really, yet they persist. I'm not the only one who feels that way. So does Bert Arvid."

"I shouldn't wonder."

"What do you mean?"

"Bert's highly perceptive, Joel."

"Perceptive to what?"

"To the fact that his reality has unreal aspects, if I can put it that way. Like you, he senses enough to be perturbed." He lifted his head. "What did Bert tell you?"

"That frightening things were happening in the world."

"Did he say what?"

"No, but he's scared."

"Of the frightening things he senses are happening, or of Department L?"

"Both," I replied promptly. "So am I."

"Do you know of anything frightening?"

"Subconsciously, yes. I have the uneasy feeling that things aren't what they should be. But don't ask me for specifics. I can't name them."

Mark's gaze lingered on my face. "I don't have to tell you that you've placed yourself in great jeopardy by coming here."

"I have a cover." I grinned. "I'm doing a series on the great names in science."

"You can't fool Department L, Joel."

"I know that, but I'm certain I wasn't followed. Or I was certain; now I'm not so sure. I'd hate to think that my trip had tipped them off." I held his gaze. "The superintendent at Arzachel told me you'd signed on for the Procellarum mines. For God's sake, why?"

"To buy time."

"Time?" I gazed uncomprehendingly at him. "Procellarum is like Arzachel, a dead-end street. Once you get there you're trapped. Neither do the men who go there come back. It's notorious."

He smiled. "We have no intention of returning."

"You fooled Department L once," I agreed, "but now that they know you're here you can't hide. Why not grab a freighter out to Mars; or better yet, to Ganymede or Titan? The farther the better. I can book your passage in my name, claim a moon marriage and book one for Ann."

"Where would that leave you, Joel?"

"I'll claim that I lost my papers, that someone must have found them and used them illegally."

He shook his head. "It wouldn't work. They'd radio ahead and we would be caught. Besides, that takes time, organization, planning. And time is what we don't have."

"So you rush into a dead-end street, is that it?"

"Perhaps we would have been as well off to remain at Arzachel," he admitted. "All we need is a short reprieve."

"I still can't understand how you hope to escape."

The ghostly smile came again. "There are other planes of human existence, Joel. I told you that."

"You've made contact?"

He nodded.

"Tell me about it," I demanded. "I have to know."

"I can't tell you any more than I have, Joel. It's something you can't comprehend without a complete understanding of the mind. Mastery of the mind, I should say. Have we words to describe the fourth or fifth or sixth or nth dimension? We can't because our words are tied to our known concepts, are limited. Do words like *infinity* and *eternity* really tell us anything? Nothing." He shook his head. "They are merely words that signal the end of our comprehension. They tell us that beyond lies the unknowable. It's something that you can't know until you experience it yourself. But our world is there, waiting."

"Then what's holding you back?"

"I am," said Ann quietly. Startled, I looked at her.

"She's gaining the mastery of her mind very rapidly," Mark broke in.

"You're waiting for her?"

"Yes, of course."

"Can't you tell me anything?" I urged.

"Nothing that can be described in terms of anything you know," replied Mark. "Nirvana, paradise, elysium—there are scores of words to describe what man has always sensed lies beyond this world, Joel. Most people, when they think of them, regard them as sort of a never-never land of the imagination, a place to be attained only in dreams. But not all. Down through the ages men have made the transition."

"How?"

"By looking inward, understanding the basic processes of the mind—the power that it holds and the ability to release that power. That power transcends time, space, physical matter. More, it controls them. But first you must believe, must perceive, must find the key to your own nature." He regarded me thoughtfully. "That key is internal, not external."

"Where is this place, the physical location?"

"On Earth, here on the moon, among the stars. It exists in the past, the present, the future. When man conquered his mind, he conquered the universe, Joel."

"So you've found it," I said thickly. "But what have you found? I'm as much in the dark as ever. What sort of life is it?"

"Man in the nearly perfect state, Joel. That is his drive —perfection."

"Can man achieve perfection? I doubt it."

"He can by correcting his errors."

A thought crept along the border of my mind, refusing to blossom into full awareness. "Correction implies back-tracking," I said finally.

"Yes." He nodded.

"Explain that, please."

He shook his head. "You'll understand some day."

"I doubt it."

"You can't attain without seeking," said Mark. "I can't tell you any more than that."

I started to pursue the subject, but saw it was useless. Mark's face held a finality. Instead, I asked, "If it's not secret, how did you slip into the identity of Fallon?"

"It wasn't difficult." He chuckled. "I planned it years ago. When I first sensed the fallacies in our concepts of reality and began probing my mind, I foresaw the possible need of a new identity. One day I read about a colonist, born on Ganymede, who died while being rushed to Earth for the treatment of a rare disease. His age was close to mine."

"You took his identity, just like that?"

"I applied for a social welfare number under his name," Mark admitted. "Having been born in the OutSats, it was normal that he had none. I needed a sponsor, of course, someone to verify my statements. Martin Wister's prestige was sufficient for that."

He explained how from time to time he'd worked under the new identity, gradually building a second analog in the computer center. It was the analog of an itinerant manual laborer. Mainly performed during the summers, the jobs had centered around mining and road construction, first in one part of the country, then in another. When the time had come for him to vanish, he'd simply surfaced under his second identity; it had been as easy as that.

"And Ann?"

"Became Mrs. Fallon. She adopted the name of a distant cousin to provide a suitable background."

"Very neat," I admitted. The ease with which he had fooled Department L delighted me.

Mark shook his head. "I'm afraid I tipped it when I called Ann through the university switchboard. I hadn't expected them to monitor that, not so soon. I terminated the call immediately, but it was too late."

"How did you know you were being monitored?" I challenged.

"Instruments." He didn't bother to explain further, nor did I ask. He continued, "We've known ever since that our time was limited, that eventually, if necessary, they'd sort through every Fallon in the world. I gambled that a miner on the moon would be about their last choice."

As we chatted, the intervals of silence grew until I realized there was no more to say. They realized it too; it showed in their faces, a certain sadness that shouted farewell. Whatever they were thinking or suffering, whatever their hopes or fears, they couldn't share them with me. In a sense they had already withdrawn from this world—were speaking to me across a gulf too great to bridge. Words were not enough. I wanted to beg Mark to reconsider, not to take Ann into the dread Oceanus Procellarum, but I didn't. I knew such a plea would be useless.

Finally I lurched to my feet. "If there's anything I can do. . . ."

"There's nothing, Joel." Ann regarded me wistfully. For the moment I almost hated Mark for having brought her there. Her life had been so filled with promise, and now. . . . I tore my eyes away. Sensing my thoughts, she said, "I'm very happy."

"I hope it lasts," I answered.

"It will." Her voice and smile held certainty. We exchanged a few more words before I turned to leave. Mark followed me outside.

"Thank you, Joel," he said softly.

"Take care of yourself, and of Ann."

"I promise that, Joel." He turned back inside and closed the door.

I was left alone.

When I returned to my room, I found a note slipped under the door. Carmody, I guessed. Something had happened. My fingers trembled as I opened it. *Must see you soonest. Arvid. Rm. 27.*

Bert Arvid! I gazed perplexedly at the message. What was the science writer doing on the moon? Why did he have to see me? *Soonest!* The word held a veiled terror.

Perhaps Carmody had to reach me, had sent Arvid rather than risk public communications. If so, it had to do with Mark Randall. Or with Department L!

I tussled indecisively with my thoughts. Would Carmody impart such knowledge to Arvid? It didn't seem likely. Arvid was Mark's friend, I knew that. But did Carmody? I doubted it. The whole affair gave me the impression of a noose being drawn ever more tightly around my neck. Or was it Mark Randall's neck? Not that there was a difference; in the eyes of Department L we both were in the same pot. I was convinced of that.

My thoughts were chaotic as I destroyed the note and went out into the corridor. Room 27 was at the far end. I knocked lightly, heard quick movement inside before the door was inched open. Bert Arvid peered worriedly through the crack before flinging it wide.

"Inside," he croaked. He gestured nervously, the fear heavy on his face.

"What's wrong?" I tried to mask my perturbation as he slammed the door behind me.

"Department L," he hissed. "Ryerson and Quinby might be here now." Ryerson and Quinby—the names clicked.

"Sparrow and Big Bull," I said. The knowledge that I was coming into the final sprint had a strangely calming effect.

"They're killers," he warned.

"Who are they after, me or Randall?"

"Both, and the girl." His attempt to smile was a dismal failure. The terror on his face gave him the look of a hunted animal. "They might be after me, too," he faltered. I tried to take the time to feel sorry for him, but couldn't. Too much was at stake.

"You warned Randall?"

"For God's sake, Joel. . . ."

"Tell me!"

"Yes," he whimpered.

I held his eyes, my mind aflame with questions. "How did you know they'd discovered where he was?"

"Don't ask me, Joel. I can't tell you that. But I came to

warn you. I don't know how you can get away but you have to try. Perhaps Mars. . . ."

"How much do they know?" I interrupted.

"They know you came to warn Randall."

"How could they know that?"

"They know," he muttered.

"Carmody?" I knew the answer as soon as I asked the question. It could only have come from him.

"Please, Joel."

"Answer me," I shouted. He jerked his head, unable to speak. His face under the lamp grew a sickly color. So, it had been Carmody! "Why did Carmody tell you?" I demanded.

"Joel, you're wasting time!"

"I have to know," I answered roughly. I liked Bert Arvid, always had, but this was no time for me to be left hanging in mid-air. When he failed to answer, I grasped his jacket and slammed him against the wall. "Talk!" I rasped.

"I've risked my neck to warn you," he cried. "Isn't that enough?"

"No!"

"You'll get us all killed, Joel."

"Spill it, Bert."

"Please. . . ." He sighed, seemed to collapse as if all the wind had gone out of him. I released him, watched him stagger to the cot and sit heavily on the edge. He looked as if he were about to weep.

"That won't do any good." I stepped forward and stood looking down at him. "I need the answers, Bert, and I'm going to get them before I leave here." I spoke with a threat although I didn't feel at all that way. Somehow Arvid had been caught in a trap. Like the rest of us, he was simply trying to escape. Yet why had he come to warn me? I flung the question at him.

He raised his head. "What difference does it make?" he asked brokenly. "We're all dead anyway."

"What makes you so certain?"

"Ryerson and Quinby—the fellows you call Sparrow

and Big Bull—do you believe they'll let anyone live who knows about Mark?"

"What about Mark?"

"What he's trying to do, Joel?"

"How much does Department L know about what he's trying to do? Do they know the whole story? Does Sparrow?"

"They know," he mumbled.

"How?"

"Frightening things are happening. I told you that before."

"What things?"

"God, Joel, you'll drive me crazy."

"Talk, Bert!"

"I don't know, I don't know," he moaned. "Things aren't like they were, although not many people seem to know that. At times I think I'm crazy, that it's all in my mind."

"Like my memory of Charles Hedron?" I asked. The question came with a flash of insight.

"Hedron!" He looked startled.

"The neo-existentialist philosopher," I explained. "I used to read him years ago, then he disappeared. None of his books are in the library, no one remembers him. But I mentioned him to Mark once. I could tell from his reaction that he recognized the name."

Arvid's eyes held a glimmer of hope. "I used to read him too, and there were others. That's what I mean, Joel. Now they're gone, gone. Something's changing the world." He looked desperately at me. "Why aren't others aware of the changes?"

"Mark said it took a special insight."

"God, what it does to the mind. I'm spooked, Joel. It's too big for me."

"It's not too big," I countered.

"But it is," he cried. "I feel like I'm splintering into a thousand parts." The hope fled from his eyes, replaced by a glassy stare. Fearing he might break down completely, I shifted tactics.

"Mark's a miner living in the pit of hell," I said. "Do

you know where he's headed? Procellarum, and he's taking Ann. He couldn't be responsible for the frightening things you say are happening."

"I didn't say that he was responsible, but he knows, understands what's happening. The world isn't ready for that kind of knowledge, Joel. The government won't allow it. We're supposed to go blindly on. To know is dangerous." He laughed hysterically.

"Talk sense," I snapped.

"The door—they're afraid he'll tell them how to open the door."

"But he won't. It's something each man must discover for himself. It's not knowledge that can be passed on, Bert. He told me that."

"But does the government know that?" He shook his head violently. "That's why they want to kill him, kill Ann. It's why they want to silence everyone who has the slightest inkling of it."

"Do you believe that such a door exists, that Mark is right?"

"I don't know," he moaned, "but if it does exist, can't you see what it means? We've been living in stasis—scientifically, socially, economically. Everything has been brought into nearly perfect balance. Input equals output. The world hasn't moved one damned bit in over a hundred years. It's a gigantic anthill, and that's the way the government wants it, Joel. But if word of Mark's beliefs got out and people even suspected he might be right, what kind of a stir do you believe that would cause? Men would have hope again. Next there would be a score of men, a hundred, a thousand working to find that door. A fever would sweep the world. A fever and a clamor and a demand that the government take this action or that. For every person fighting to open the door, another would be fighting to keep it closed. Do you believe the government wants that?"

"Do you want it?"

"No, it frightens me. I'm of this world, this time. I couldn't take the shock of knowing I was nothing, and that's what it would amount to."

"Yet you warned him, gave him his chance to escape. Why?"

"I have to live with myself, Joel." His eyes pleaded with me. "I'm caught in a trap, have been caught too long. I've been a puppet dancing on a string. Don't you believe I want to be a man?"

"I'm not condemning you, Bert."

"You should," he muttered.

"Why?"

"Please. . . ." His face torn with anguish, he looked to be in the depths of despair. I wanted to feel sorry for him, but couldn't. For all his knowledge he was a weak reed caught in forces too great for him.

I asked, "Why did Carmody confide in you? How are you tied up in all this, Bert?"

"Joel," he moaned.

"Talk," I commanded. "We haven't much time."

"Don't you know by now, Joel? The *Solar Press* is the eyes and ears of Department L, has been for the last half a dozen years. It was taken over at Karl Burger's personal orders."

"Burger!" I recoiled a step. Karl Burger, the director of the BPS. . . . My thoughts were in turmoil. "Why would the *Solar Press* bow to Burger?" I demanded.

"Burger's men bought in through fronts until they controlled the stock, then placed their men in key places."

"Harvey Sinclair?" I rasped.

"Harvey wouldn't go along with them."

"So they killed him," I said harshly. "Carmody?"

He nodded lifelessly.

"How do you know all that?" I already knew the answer but asked anyway. He lifted his head, his eyes stricken. "You were part of it," I charged.

"I couldn't help it, Joel. I was talking to Carmody—oh, that was months before Harvey's death—when I happened to mention Mark's beliefs. It was just a passing remark but he seized on it, ordered me to find out exactly what Mark was doing."

"Why didn't you take it to Sinclair at the time?"

"Carmody warned me that it was a Department L matter, that I would be held accountable if the information got out. Several frightening things already had happened that someone else remembered. Things like Charles Hedron's disappearance. Department L had caught wind of them and was greatly excited. When they got the tip on Mark, they reasoned that there might be a relationship. Whatever it was, it set them on his track. I know that Karl Burger personally is directing the investigation."

He gazed forlornly at me. "Later, when I couldn't stand what I was doing, I tipped Harvey anonymously, but by then it was too late. He started to investigate it as a straight news story but when he was ordered to attack Randall he couldn't stand the pressure. He rebelled; that's when he died."

"Murdered," I said harshly.

"Yes, murdered."

"So now you're trying to whitewash your conscience, is that it?"

"I came to warn you. I've put my life on the line."

"All right, Bert." I struggled to get my emotions under control. Arvid, normally a decent man, simply had fallen into a trap in which far bigger men might have buckled just as easily. Perhaps I would have folded the same way. Still, I had to find out what he knew.

I studied him dispassionately. "How do you know that Sparrow and Big Bull are on the moon?"

"Ryerson and Quinby? Carmody told me. I used my press credential to hop a freighter on the pretext of doing a story. Perhaps I beat them; I don't know."

"Does Carmody know you're here?"

"God, I hope not." He shuddered.

"You said that the department would kill anyone who knew Mark's secret. Is that true?"

"Except for perhaps the highest echelon of government," he replied miserably.

"Why would they except Carmody?"

"I believe he's Karl Burger's man."

"Stooge to the head policeman, is that it?"

Arvid shifted uneasily. "He doesn't seem afraid."

"Why would they except you?"

"I don't know," he blurted.

"Think about it, Bert. If the secret's as dangerous as you say, why should they let you live? They've already murdered Martin Wister, Harvey Sinclair, and God alone knows how many others. So why should they let anyone live once he's served his purpose?"

"I've thought of that. I've tried to buy my life by cooperating. I've been a coward, a fool, now I'm trying to redeem myself." Hope flared in his face again as he rushed on, "I don't believe anyone knows of my connection except Carmody. He might not talk."

"You're living in a fool's paradise," I snapped. I felt like a sadist as he recoiled from my words. At the same time I felt a brief glimmer of hope. An organization like Department L must certainly be built on the old cell principle, with each cell operating as a self-contained unit. While it got its instructions from the cell above, the *modus operandi* was strictly its own. On that basis it was possible, barely possible, that no one knew of my own involvement except Carmody, Sparrow, and Big Bull. And Bert. If I could kill the two agents, go back and kill Carmody. . . .

Good God, now I was thinking of murder! I had to laugh, but the thought remained. Why not? The will to survive was a response nature had placed in its first life-form perhaps a billion years before. That response had been an integral part of life ever since. Survival per se towered above any consideration of the means. Men followed that principle; so did nations—right down the primrose path to self-destruction.

But I had to act. For whatever good it might do, I had to warn Mark and Ann, give them their chance, then grab a freighter for Mars, Ganymede, lonely Titan. Do that or sign up for the mines of Oceanus Procellarum. Not that Department L wouldn't track me, but I could make it tough.

My gaze returned to Bert. Sitting on the cot with his face buried in his hands, he appeared like a doomed man awaiting his executioner. Perhaps he was. Perhaps we both were. But I intended to go down fighting.

"Stay where you are," I warned. "Keep out of sight. I'll be right back."

"Where are you going?" He rose, his face taut with apprehension.

"I can't tell you, Bert. It's too dangerous."

"Take care of yourself, Joel." He tried a smile. I peered into the corridor, saw it was empty, and hurriedly left. As I crossed the central depot, I thought of death. I don't know why, but I did.

My mind screamed with it.

TEN

The tunnel which housed Mark's cabin appeared darker and more tortuous than ever. Pale lamps cast bizarre shadows on the walls. Fetid and heavy, the air lay sickly in my lungs. I couldn't imagine that the living quarters of the Procellarum mines could be worse.

Here and there I glimpsed the same huddled figures as before, heard the same whispery voices. In my imagination, each shadow became a Department L agent, watching and gloating as I hurried to my doom. Where better a place to murder a man? The thought brought a cold sweat. By the time I reached the cabin my nerves were fairly crackling.

My knock brought quick movement from inside. The door was flung open and Mark stepped out to meet me. "Department L?" he asked quietly.

"Coming or already here." I didn't bother to whisper. "I just saw Bert Arvid. He came to warn you."

"He's already warned me." Mark smiled faintly.

"To emphasize what he's already told you," I put in hurriedly. I tersely revealed the gist of what Arvid had said without revealing his role in the affair. If Mark guessed the truth, he didn't let on.

"Wait," he instructed briefly. He returned inside before I could answer. His lack of perturbation and his apparent preparation for just such an emergency brought me a sense of assurance that caused the tension to drain from my body. I felt, for the first time, a real spark of hope. Yet what could he do? I juggled the question perplexedly.

He reappeared shortly, followed by Ann. This time their rough clothing had been replaced by quite presentable garments, the kind worn by administrative personnel and the occasional visitors who came to the moon to gain the status of space travel. I guessed they had hoarded them for just such a time. Mark reached back, flipped off the light, and shut the door.

"Where to?" I asked worriedly.

"Procellarum."

"You might have to wait in the station for hours."

"I don't believe so."

"But. . . ." I started to argue, instead clamped my jaws shut. This was Mark's show. Whatever he hoped to accomplish had been thought out long since. I saw that in his face and demeanor. He was moving with purpose toward an already selected goal.

I glanced at Ann. Her face, half-hidden in the shadows, didn't appear unduly worried. I had to marvel at her composure, yet realized it was founded in complete trust in Mark. She caught my look and smiled reassuringly.

As Mark led us back through the tunnel, I clasped Ann's hand. While we picked our way past the squat plastic cabins, past spectral knots of men who whispered in the darkness, a thousand questions danced in my mind. If Mark actually had managed to contact another plane of existence, how did he hope to make the actual transition? Teleportation? No, he'd said it was something different. What? Although his explanations as far as he had gone were too vague to be called explanatory, I was convinced he knew exactly what he was doing. So was Ann.

Posed against what he'd told me was my own concept of the universe, of time. Any other was all but unthinkable. Yet I had to admit that many things had happened in history for which there were no plausible explanations. And I'd read Charles Hedron's philosophy. Much of it remained quite clear in my mind, even after the years. All the librarians in the world could scream that such a writer had never existed, but I knew better. So did Bert Arvid and Mark Randall. Especially Mark Randall.

So if there had been a Charles Hedron? I let the question run through my mind. The corollary was that a suitable explanation had to reach beyond anything I knew, beyond the concepts so deeply ingrained in my mind. I had to consider other planes of human existence. I could well understand Bert Arvid's turmoil.

Mark paused at the mouth of the tunnel to scan the cavernous depot beyond. A group of men were drifting across the main floor. The few other figures discernible appeared innocuous enough. Finally he gestured and struck out toward the terminus which housed the monorail line that serviced the mines of Oceanus Procellarum.

In a lull between runs, it was all but deserted. Only three men were visible. Two worked with forklifts; a third was puttering around an ugly rectangular gondola of the type that had carried me to Crater Arzachel.

I took in the remainder of the station with a sweeping glance. Boxes, bales, coils of wire, pressure bottles—it was piled high with cargo. Parked against a wall were several land rovers of the type used to work on the lunar surface. Their domed compartments, although dwarfed by the huge doughnut-shaped wheels, were sufficiently large to carry a considerable load in addition to four or five men. I felt no prickling of the scalp, detected nothing of a threatening nature, yet that in itself set my teeth on edge. I was tight with anticipation.

The man working on the gondola straightened at our approach, his eyes speculative. He didn't bother with Ann or me, but riveted his gaze directly on Mark. In truth, we were slight shadows compared with the scientist's gigantic figure. His shock of flaming hair commanded attention. More than that, his manner screamed of authority. Despite my edginess, I had to admire him.

Mark walked past him with eloquent disregard and casually opened the gondola door. He took the time to inspect the vehicle thoroughly before turning back. "Who's in charge here?" he barked.

"I am." The worker stepped forward, his manner suddenly deferent. "I'm the station attendant," he added.

Mark glared at him. "Why haven't you loaded one of the land rovers?"

The attendant gazed perplexedly at him. "I haven't had orders to that effect."

"They were sent down," snapped Mark. "Headquarters requested one for the inspection."

"Inspection?"

"Of Procellarum. Don't you keep track of orders?"

"Yes, sir, but. . . ."

"Hurry," Mark interrupted impatiently, "we have a schedule to meet."

"Yes, sir." The attendant shouted nervously to one of the forklift operators. The latter turned his vehicle toward us, its engine rising to a high whine. The two conversed briefly before the vehicle rolled toward one of the doughnut-wheeled cargo carriers.

The attendant entered the gondola. A moment later a cable-controlled door at the rear swung outward and down, its lip coming to rest on the floor to form a ramp. Mark watched the proceedings stonily.

The forklift operator transferred to a land rover. As its engine purred to life, he guided it forward, inched it up the ramp into the gondola. When it was blocked in place, the ramp was drawn up into a sealed position to keep the interior airtight during the long dash across the lunar surface.

When the attendant emerged from the gondola, Mark collared him. "Load two space suits and a maximum supply of oxygen," he barked.

"Yes, sir." The attendant shouted the order. Despite the gravity of our situation, I had to smile at Mark's audacity. He appeared for all the world like the archetype of executive authority. The attendant must have believed so too, for his additional orders were obeyed with alacrity. Once Mark winked at me.

"We are what we say we are," he murmured.

"Until the real boss comes," I whispered back. He laughed. But I knew he was right. Despite the cynicism of the human animal, he's prone to take people at face value, at least until he learns differently. In a sense we all are

actors, hiding behind our roles. Or perhaps it is more
correct to say that the role is used as a tool of achievement. Whatever it is, Mark portrayed his role superbly. I
wished I could say the same about myself.

When the work was finished, he leaned toward me.
"You'd better leave, Joel." I shook my head, determined to
see it through. He strolled to the gondola, opened the cab
door, and beckoned to Ann.

"Good-bye, and thank you," she murmured. She
squeezed my hand before hurrying to join him.

"Good-bye," I called. All at once I was filled with nervous fear. The station attendant eyed them uncertainly as
they slid into the vehicle. I could see him struggling with
his indecision. The forklift operators were watching curiously. The moment was heavy with suspense.

Mark leaned from the cab. "Man the airlock," he called.
His voice rang with authority. The station attendant looked
helplessly at me and I nodded. As if that confirmed Mark's
prerogatives, he disappeared into the control booth.

Gripped by a sudden anxiety, I hurried toward the
gondola. Mark opened the door. "This is crazy," I hissed.
"When they discover what has happened, they'll contact
Procellarum. You'll find a reception committee."

"No." He shook his head and smiled.

"What do you hope to gain?"

"Life, Joel."

"What kind of life, for God's sake?"

"We'll be among our kind."

"You know that?"

"Absolutely."

"Please don't worry about us," Ann counseled.

"I still have to know," I insisted. "You just can't rush off
to Procellarum. I have to know what's ahead for you. I
can't end my days wondering."

Mark said, "Perhaps some day. . . ."

"Some day what?" I interrupted.

"You might find your own door, Joel."

"Never!" I laughed harshly. "I'm Homo sapien Model
2230 A.D. I live in the here and now and that's it."

"You have a rare gift," he countered.

"Gift?"

"A memory that now and then perceives through time," he explained. "It's quite unusual."

"Sure, I can think of last year, this year and next year, if that's what you mean."

"I'm serious, Joel." His eyes rested keenly on me. "Remember you spoke of Charles Hedron and his neo-existentialist philosophy?"

Gazing at him I tried to follow his meaning. Sure, I'd spoken of Hedron during our first interview—the man whose books I couldn't find. All at once something stood still in my mind, something crazy and yet quite logical. "What about Hedron?" I asked.

"He didn't exist, Joel." He shook his head. "Not in the reality you know."

"That doesn't make sense," I cried, but my words were hollow.

"You have a gift."

"But he was here!"

"In a reality the world no longer knows."

"Put it into English, Mark. I have to know."

"Charles Hedron was here before the readjusted past. But in the readjustment he was eliminated, probably to prevent certain trends that his thinking had started. Now it's just as if he had never been here. That's your gift, Joel —the ability to remember events which occurred before the readjustment. It's like looking into another time plane."

Readjusted! As the word struck home, an enormous suspicion staggered my mind. *"Frightening things are happening in the world"*—Bert Arvid's words rushed back, smashing at me like a giant hammer. I was groping with the new comprehension when I saw Mark reach for the door.

"Good-bye, Joel," he said. "Give our best to Bert."

"Wait," I cried.

"I'll be back."

"You will?" Startled, I gazed at him.

"In a sense, yes. In time you'll put the bits and pieces

together, Joel. You're very good at that. One day you'll know. But we have to hurry. Time is short."

"Take care of yourselves."

"Good-bye," Ann called softly, "and thank you, Joel."

Mark closed the door, peered out through the glass and waved. Ann's face held a gay smile that didn't quite come off. Half-choked with emotion, I stepped back as the doors to the airlock slid open. Despite Mark's enigmatic promise to return, I knew I was seeing them for the last time. The knowledge brought a great sadness.

A low purring filled the terminus as the gondola rolled forward on its overhead rail. As the lock closed behind it, a light flashed to indicate the opening of the outer door. A faint vibration came through the floor as the gondola slid out into the long upward-slanting tunnel that would carry it to the moon's airless surface.

"Before the readjusted past"—gazing at the empty lock, I let the words swirl through my mind. Charles Hedron, the neo-existentialist philosopher had existed in my time, yet he hadn't—that was the essence of Mark's words. Hedron, his books, his influence, everything was gone—everything except the memory of him that lingered in my mind. But if he'd never lived in this reality there'd be no memory, for he wouldn't have existed. I couldn't have remembered him. But I had, hence my memory had pierced another reality!

How could that be? A rare gift, Mark Randall had called it. That's why the librarians and others had looked blank when I'd inquired about his works; I was inquiring about a man who had never existed in their time, or in their history. God! I rubbed my temples.

"Something frightening is happening in the world." I thought of Bert Arvid's words again. Arvid, too, had the gift. Like me, he'd remembered men only to find that they'd never existed. Small wonder he believed he might be crazy. Only he knew that he wasn't crazy. He knew that it had something to do with Mark Randall and the door and time.

But Arvid and I weren't alone! Someone else with that

rare gift had sensed the same thing, had started Karl Burger on the investigation which, finally, had centered on Mark. It was wild and crazy and illogical, except that I had proof.

I remembered Charles Hedron!

My chain of thought was broken as the station attendant came toward me from the control booth. "Who did that fellow say he was?" he asked indecisively.

"You don't know?" I eyed him askance. "He's the vice president."

"Of what?"

"Mine inspection." I spun on my heel before he could speak and hurried across the cavernous room. That Mark's ruse would not go long undetected appeared a certainty. Yet Mark had known that. I couldn't imagine that his flight was one of desperation; he'd appeared too calm. So had Ann. What would happen next? The question baffled me.

At the far side of the depot, I glanced back. Still standing where I'd left him, the station attendant was scratching his head.

Bert Arvid was gone!

My heartbeat rose to a fast hammer as I gazed into the cubicle where I'd left him. Empty, with the light still burning, it contained the few personal articles I'd noticed earlier. My first surmise that he had panicked and had made a run for it vanished as I realized there was no place for him to run. Not on the moon.

Where could he be? I eyed the room uneasily, the fear forming a clump in my throat. Sparrow! I felt cold as the agent's thin visage flashed into my mind. The mild blue eyes seemed to mock me. Instinctively I knew that somehow Sparrow was responsible for Bert Arvid's disappearance.

Slowly retreating from the room, I glanced both ways along the corridor, saw no one. The best move I could make was to get away, get back to Earth—forget that Mark Randall and Ann Willett had ever existed. But I couldn't run; I was too deeply committed, the more so because of Bert Arvid. When Sparrow caught him, if he hadn't already, Arvid would talk readily enough. Big Bull would see to that.

As the degree of my involvement struck me, I felt a panic. The superintendent of Baker Mining was one witness to my interest in Mark Randall alias Fallon; the station attendant was another. The latter was particularly damning. Nothing that I might say could explain that.

And there was Ed Carmody! How I hoped to cope with him, I didn't know. There was no way out, not for me. The realization brought a cold sweat. Joel Blake, pigeon, and the guns were up. I had to run, run, run. Only it was too late to run. I'd used up all my running space.

The Solar System was simply too small.

Outside the door to my room, I felt the hair prickle at the nape of my neck. Danger signals screamed in my mind. It was exactly the same sensation I'd had when Sparrow & Company had taken me in tow outside my apartment. The smell of death was heavy in my nostrils. Death and fear.

Trembling, I suppressed the desire to flee. My only recourse was to stand steady, brazen the situation out, try to sell an attitude of cooperation. With a sick feeling I opened the door, fully expecting to find the two agents waiting. I was wrong.

Instead I found Bert Arvid.

The laser burn that ran like a trench above his eyes told me he was dead. Dead, but the eyes were open, bulging horribly. I took several steps toward him, then stopped. Dead, in my room! The implication struck me like a sledge. Someone had set me up for a murder rap! I was gazing at the body when a noise behind me brought me violently around.

Sparrow was watching me from the doorway.

ELEVEN

"Well, well, another murder." Sparrow walked past me and gazed down at Bert Arvid's body. Murder! He'd called it that before he'd even had a chance to see the manner of Arvid's death, or whether or not there might be a gun in Arvid's hand. I could only gaze stupidly at him, feel the fear and anger boil in my chest.

He turned casually. "You appear to have quite a propensity for finding murder victims, Blake. Or did you manufacture this one?"

"I just came in," I retorted hotly. "You must have seen me."

"True, but weren't you here earlier?"

"He wasn't in my room when I left."

"But you saw him earlier?" He watched me sharply. I started to deny it, then realized he probably knew all about my meeting with Arvid—most likely had every word taped. If so, he knew Mark Randall's destination. Yet, if that were so, why hadn't he moved to stop him? Or had he gotten the information from Arvid too late? "Well?" he asked testily.

"I saw him," I admitted.

"What did you talk about?"

"Story ideas."

"Ah!" Sparrow sighed gently.

"What's so unusual about that?"

His face hardened. "Why did you come to the moon, Blake?"

"The same reason, a story."

"The Famous Names in Science series, eh?"

"That was part of it."

"You came to warn Mark Randall alias Ray Fallon," he corrected. "I know all about it, Blake."

"I'd heard he was here," I acknowledged. "I was trying to contact him, yes."

"And did you?"

"I got here too late. He was gone."

"How about the Willett girl? Or should I call her Mrs. Fallon?"

"She was gone, too."

"Lies, all lies," exclaimed Sparrow softly.

"Why should I lie?" I protested. "You knew I was searching for Randall. I never denied it."

"You're wasting your time, Blake." He gestured toward Arvid's body. "How do you explain that?"

"How do *you* explain it?" I gritted. Quite suddenly I knew I had to kill him, had to return to Earth and kill Ed Carmody. It was my only chance. Murder leads to murder—the thought was sickening.

"I'm in the fortunate position of not having to make explanations," replied Sparrow. Instinctively I stiffened as the thought of murder pounded at my mind. His hand darted inside his jacket pocket, came out with a wicked-looking laser. He held it indolently. "Don't try it, Blake."

"I have no such intention."

The gentle smile came again. "I'm certain that such a thought never entered your mind. But what are you thinking, Blake? Perhaps you're pondering what lies ahead. I shouldn't wonder that you're worried." He was playing with me and I knew it. More, it was the sadistic kind of play that suddenly I realized he enjoyed. The knowledge was infuriating. I wanted to shout that I knew all about the *Solar Press*, about Ed Carmody and Bert Arvid, about the web of death being spun by Department L in the effort to kill Mark Randall. What held me back was the knowledge that it would give him greater satisfaction, if only because it would point up my own despair.

Footsteps outside brought my eyes up nervously. Big Bull halted, framed in the doorway. His small pig eyes never bothered with Bert Arvid's body; then went directly from me to Sparrow. Gesturing, he retreated a few yards and Sparrow followed. They held a whispered conversation before Sparrow swung back.

"Come with us." He gestured with the laser.

"Why should I?"

"You're under arrest for murder, Blake."

"How could I have shot him?" I demanded. "I haven't a gun."

"You dumped it," replied Sparrow. "Now come along."

"If I refuse?"

"You'll remain here a long, long time." He pointed the weapon lazily in my direction. Glowering at him, I knew I was beat. If I refused, they'd burn me down where I stood. Big Bull struck me as the man who'd relish the job. In the end, I nodded jerkily. They stepped aside as I left the room, then followed close behind.

"Where are we going?" I demanded.

"The terminus to Procellarum," answered Sparrow. "I'm certain you're acquainted with the place. It's where the vice presidents hop off on their inspection tours."

"Very funny," I gritted.

"Quite humorous," he agreed. "I can understand why you're a writer. Ever try your hand at fiction? I believe you'd be quite good at it." I didn't answer.

As we crossed the central depot, I noted a dozen or so figures milling around in the previously all but deserted terminus. Another gondola had been swung onto the main rail and a land rover was being loaded aboard. Plainly Big Bull had been busy in the short time that had elapsed.

That Sparrow intended to pursue Mark Randall was evident. Yet I wondered why. He could have radioed ahead, had Randall and Ann returned under guard. Or did he consider Oceanus Procellarum a more ideal place for murder?

As we drew nearer, a figure darted toward us. It was the station attendant. "That's the man," he cried. He jabbed a finger toward me. "That's the fellow who told me the big red-haired one was a vice president."

"He seems to know you," observed Sparrow. He eyed

me reproachfully. I didn't answer. Disregarding the station attendant, Sparrow gestured me toward the gondola. Big Bull spoke to one of the men, who a moment later I saw loading space gear—the kind you wear to romp around on the surface of the moon. The sight wasn't reassuring.

Sparrow herded me into the gondola, beckoned me to a seat and went out again. As the ramp closed behind me and I sat alone in my cocoon of light metal and leaded glass, I worried about what lay ahead. Somewhere on the bleak lunar plains, far to the west, Mark and Ann were speeding toward Oceanus Procellarum, the desolate Ocean of Storms, from which there could be no escape. Certainly a reception committee would be waiting for the gondola to appear. Yet Mark, anticipating that probability, had chosen it as his path of flight. Despite Mark's confidence, I remained painfully aware that he was still the hunted, Sparrow the hunter.

My attention was jerked back as the agents entered the gondola. Big Bull swept past me and sat in the rear. I noticed, as he passed, that he kept a hand inside his jacket. Sparrow moved to the small compartment that housed the simple controls.

He closed the cab door, took a dial reading on airtight security, and turned a switch. A low humming came, together with the stir of air from a circulation fan. As the inner doors of the airlock rolled open, the engine of the gondola purred to life.

The gondola passed into the lock, halted, and the doors behind us closed. An instant later the forward doors rolled open with a hiss as the air from the lock exploded outward into the vacuum of the tube.

A blinking red light ahead changed to green. The gondola moved forward, gathering speed as it rushed along the slanting tunnel that led to the surface of the moon. The black walls rushing past me, the pale lights in the vehicle, Sparrow peering ahead through the leaded port—the situation gave me an odd feeling of unreality, as if it were something I was sensing in a dream. But it wasn't a dream. A nightmare, perhaps, but not a dream.

"Do you think they'll let anyone live who knows about Mark?" The wretched look on Bert Arvid's face came to life in my mind as I recalled his warning. He'd known that he was as good as dead; that had been his terror.

Now I was slated to die!

The knowledge was unnerving but true. Martin Wister, Harvey Sinclair, Bert Arvid, and next—Joel Blake! I had to smile crookedly at the certainty. But why hadn't they killed me already?

It would be neater to do it on the lunar surface, I reflected. The murder of Bert Arvid in the Sinus Medii could be pinned on me neatly enough, but two murders might start rumors. Sparrow was craftsman enough to realize that. A murder on the lonely surface was something else again. Dumped into a convenient rift or pothole, the victim could lie undisturbed for a thousand, a million years. In the airless vacuum, he could stare into the black lunar skies until the end of eternity.

"I'll be back." Mulling Mark's words, I tried to fathom what he had meant. He'd said that in time I'd put the bits and pieces together, know the whole story. Because I had the ability to see through time? I couldn't, I knew that, if I excepted the single instance in which I'd remembered a man who hadn't existed *in this reality.* Yet he had existed; Mark had acknowledged that. *Before the readjusted past!*

I knew what he'd meant but couldn't believe it. And yet I could. I could believe it because Mark Randall believed it. And Ann Willett. And I could believe it because Karl Burger, the director of the BPS, had turned his dread Department L to the task of silencing everyone who knew about it. That, as much as anything else, convinced me.

Abruptly the gondola burst from the mouth of the tunnel into the bright lunar day. The cooling system groaned as it sought to counter the 250 degree heat into which the vehicle had plunged. I saw that we were streaking upward toward the stark ridges that formed the western boundary of the Sinus Medii.

I turned to glance back. Big Bull, as immobile as a statue, had his small piggish eyes riveted directly on me.

They held the curious unseeing quality of the blind. "Nice to be out in the open," I observed.

He didn't answer. Turning back, I gazed ahead through the leaded glass, tried to keep from thinking how it would be to lie out on that desolate surface for all eternity to come. They say it makes no difference to the dead where they lie. Although that might be true on Earth, I didn't have the same feelings about the moon. Yet men were born and died on Mars, on Ganymede, on Titan. But that wasn't for me. I was strictly an earthling.

Men among the stars, men who mastered time—Mark's statements echoed like little bells in the dim corridors of my mind. Who was to say what was probable and what was improbable? What did I really know about the universe, about time, about life itself? Very little, when I contemplated it. I'd been born into a set of facts which in turn had become my reality. Facts, when called laws, no longer were questioned. Except by the Mark Randalls of the world. And the Ann Willetts. To them, the facts crumpled like paper houses in a storm. Yet men had to have an anchor. That's what baffled me.

I was losing my anchor.

The gondola rushed into a gorge and instantly the world was black. The temperature controls groaned anew under a minus 240 degree cold. In the airless vacuum through which we sped, the geometry of light and shadow was one of stark contrast—blinding light or jet black, with none of the pleasing gradations brought by the diffusion of light in an atmosphere.

I had the eerie impression of swinging in pitch and yaw, the vertiginous sensation of swerving, climbing, dropping with such rapidity that all motion congealed into one. Up between the walls of the black canyon I saw a thin swath of stars. Then the gondola burst out into the harsh light again.

With the sun midway to the horizon, the desolate plain ahead and far below was a formless pattern of light and shadow. Bizarre rock formations jutted like lonely sentinels into the sky. Wild, beautiful, fearsome—it was easy to see what had drawn men to the moon. A certain kind of men, I reflected. They were men who, in the olden days, would have been guiding wagon trains across the great western deserts—men with adventure and curiosity and courage. The moon wasn't for city dwellers.

I twisted my head to gaze upward. The Earth, in its quarter-phase, was gigantic. A golden tan, wrapped in a halo, it commanded the heavens. Had men been created first on the moon, the Earth certainly would have been their goal.

Because the moon rotated on its axis in precisely the same time it took to complete a single orbit, the Earth never rose nor set, but hung perpetually above the moon's visible face. Although it passed through phases as the sun's angle changed, it never vanished from sight. Even when "new"—when the Earth lay between the sun and the moon with its darkened face moonward—the halo formed by its atmosphere was as visible as a thin ring of silvery light. Watched throughout the two-week long days and nights, the Earth would move in a small circle about its own average position, but that was all. From the bleak ridges over which the gondola sped, the Earth forever held the center of the celestial stage.

The sight brought a nostalgia that made me jerk away my eyes. Would I ever again see a tropical beach, or the towers of San Francisco caught in a fog? It was agonizing to think that I might not.

The gondola curved downward through a vast stone canyon, past jagged spires of a coppery hue set against the velvet sky. It was a lithic wonderland of which the Earth had no equal. With no wind to blow, no rain to fall, no green life to thrive, the entire beauty was that of rock alone—rock and the black velvet sky.

The canyon walls swept to the rear as we sped out onto an immense, featureless plain. Ahead and to both sides it stretched seemingly into infinity. And yet it wasn't quite featureless. Here and there were rifts, craterlets, pocks, slabs of rock canted at crazy angles. And there was coal-black shadows. Always shadows.

As we plunged westward almost astride the lunar equator, I desperately tried to evolve a plan of action. Each idea was rejected almost as quickly as it occurred. How could I plan when the future was absolutely unforeseeable? That was my predicament. In the end I gave up, but I didn't surrender hope.

Morosely I watched the plain unfold through the leaded glass in front of Sparrow. Somewhere, far ahead, sped the gondola which carried Mark and Ann. I wondered at their hopes and fears and plans—or had they a plan? Almost certainly they had, for it was inconceivable that Mark should move without knowing exactly what he was doing. He knew but I didn't; that was the damnable part of it. I could only see his flight as the height of futility.

But if Mark and Ann were rushing to their doom, so was I. Death screamed in my mind! It wasn't the feel of death that I'd known when I'd gazed down at the body of Martin Wister, at Bert Arvid. This was the feel of personal death. It lay like an icy finger in my brain. The question wasn't *if* it would happen, but *when*, and *where*. It didn't help to know that the bullish agent behind me probably could have given me the answer.

For what seemed hours I watched the plain sweep past. Although my scant knowledge of the moon mainly had derived from maps, I was able to judge the gondola's progress by some of the better-known landmarks. The seven-sided crater Gambart, wheeling past on the right, and the jagged range of hills that followed told me we were almost halfway to our destination.

I sweated every foot of it.

I wondered what Sparrow and Big Bull thought of the man in the fleeing gondola ahead. The question intrigued me. Were they operating in full knowledge of Randall's quest, or were they simply responding to orders, with no real knowledge of who or what Mark Randall might be? Perhaps no one except Karl Burger and a few higher-ups knew the real story. And Ed Carmody; I couldn't forget Ed Carmody.

Abruptly Sparrow jerked erect, a soft exclamation escaping his lips. Alerted, I leaned forward to peer over his shoulder. Far ahead, hanging motionless from its rail, was a silver gondola. I felt a quick trepidation, at the same time sensing the tug of inertial forces that told me our own vehicle was decelerating.

"What's happening?" I asked edgily. It was a foolish question that no one bothered to answer. Inadvertently I glanced back; Big Bull's face was as expressionless and immobile as before. But the small eyes, watchful, weren't pinned on me; they were pinned on the scene ahead. I calculated the distance between us, looked at the hand in his jacket, and sighed; Big Bull couldn't be taken that easily.

As I swung back, I was startled at how quickly we were spanning the distance between the two gondolas. With only a few hundred yards to go, I saw that the rear ramp of the other vehicle had been lowered; the gondola was empty. My eyes swept the plain; it, too, was empty.

Sparrow allowed the gondola to glide to within a few yards of the other vehicle before bringing it to a halt. As he did, I glimpsed the wide tracks of a land rover pointed into the north toward the low range of mountains dominated by crater Kepler. North into nothingness; north into a desolation still untouched by man. Why? The question tore frantically at my mind. Even with ample oxygen supplies the land rover's cooling system couldn't hold up for more than eight or ten hours at most.

I brought my gaze back to Sparrow. Studying the tracks, he lifted his head to squint into the north. "It's the end of the line for Randall and the babe," he observed matter-of-factly.

"Perhaps." I forced the denial, even though I privately had to agree with him.

"We intend to make certain." He nodded to Big Bull, who brought out a laser gun. I started to sweat until I saw that he was just holding it as a precautionary measure.

Sparrow pawed through several compartments, found a piece of wire and wrapped one end around the trigger of his own weapon. The other end he fashioned into a loop.

Finished, he laid the weapon carefully beside him, struggled into one of the space suits, then picked it up again.

This time I saw the reason for the loop at the end of the wire. The index finger of the gloved hand was much too big to fit under the trigger guard; it did fit nicely into the loop. All Sparrow had to do was hold the weapon and yank back on the wire. Very neat. I had to admire his thinking.

Big Bull doctored his weapon in the same way before struggling into his space gear. When he finished, Sparrow gestured to me to take the remaining suit. It took us several minutes to figure how to connect the portable oxygen units, activate the suit transmitters, and activate the temperature controls we'd need if we had to leave the land rover.

With the suits inflated, Sparrow bled the air from the gondola and turned a switch to lower the rear ramp while Big Bull freed the land rover from its moorings. First to enter the vehicle, he took the rearmost seat. He held the laser gun clasped lazily, his index finger hooked through the wire loop.

At his nod, I sat immediately in front of him. Sparrow sat in the driver's seat and fiddled with the controls. The engine purred to life and the big doughnut-wheeled vehicle backed down the ramp and out onto the lunar plain.

Sparrow pointed it into the north, following the tracks left by Mark's vehicle. If the lunar surface had appeared bleak from the gondola, it looked a hundred times more so from the land rover. Each ridge and rift and pock had either to be circled or lumbered across with maddening slowness, all of which added to my impression of the vastness and utter desolation of the land. I had the impression of riding a beetle into an immensity too great to comprehend.

I tried to keep from thinking what might happen in the minutes or hours ahead. What would Sparrow do when he spotted the other vehicle? My suspicions of what he might try to do brought a clammy sweat. I said "try" because I'd resolved that he wouldn't do it. If I had to die, I'd take Sparrow & Company with me. I swore a silent oath on that.

Several times the tracks in the crunchy soil vanished, only to reappear farther to the north. After a while it became apparent that Mark wasn't trying to elude pursuit, for he didn't bother to seek the rock-hard ground that left no tracks. Neither did he deviate from his northern course. Did he know where he was headed? I couldn't imagine that he did.

As the cabin temperature grew hotter, Sparrow adjusted the controls. I can't say that it did much good. The sweat stung my eyes, half blinding me. Beyond the leaded glass, the lunar landscape became a blur. My only satisfaction was that I wasn't alone in my misery. Watching Sparrow squirm uncomfortably, I had to laugh.

Finally he studied his gages and glanced back at Big Bull. "We're almost at the point of no return," he said. "Randall couldn't get back if he wanted to."

"Keep going," replied Big Bull. Startled, I looked at him. It was the first time I'd heard him speak.

"You talk," I exclaimed. As he stared stolidly at me, I swung back to Sparrow. "Don't listen to him. Turn back before it's too late," I urged.

Sparrow shook his head. "If he says go, we go."

"If *he* says?"

"He gives the orders."

"Big Bull?" I blurted.

"Inspector-agent Quinby," replied Sparrow stiffly. I turned to gaze disbelievingly at Big Bull. His eyes were blank again.

As the land rover breasted a small ridge, I caught a glint in the distance that reminded me of sunlight reflected off a windowpane. My heart thumped like a drop hammer. Sparrow caught it too. Straining forward, he peered through the leaded glass. "Up ahead," he said tersely.

Big Bull shifted to look over my shoulder. I had the wild impulse to attempt to wrest the laser gun from his grasp, but as quickly realized the futility of it. He could burn me down before I could get started. Or would he risk loosing a laser beam in the interior of the land rover?

I debated it uneasily. One stray beam touching the plexi-dome would instantly destroy the vehicle's airtight integrity. If that happened we were dead; the suits alone could never sustain us until we reached the gondola. Did Big Bull realize that? I couldn't believe he was that bright.

Against that, my time was running short—short for Mark and Ann as well. Whatever move I made had to be made soon. I tossed the idea around restlessly. Still, Sparrow or Big Bull couldn't use a laser against the other vehicle without first decompressing, getting outside. I hadn't considered that before. Not that the knowledge helped, but it did give me an excuse for prolonging action.

Gazing intently ahead, I caught the glint again. This time I placed it as the reflection of light off a plexidome. In short time the vehicle took form. Against the infinity beyond, it appeared stationary. Sparrow realized it too.

"Stalled," he said. The words were a death knell in my ears. Hunched forward in his seat, Sparrow pushed the land rover to maximum speed. It rose and fell over the uneven surface like a small boat in the tides. As the vehicle ahead grew closer and closer, I knew we'd reached the end of the road. I glanced back at Big Bull. He was holding the laser pointed directly at me.

"Suit pressure," rasped Sparrow. He closed his face-plate without taking his eyes from the scene ahead. I numbly followed suit, turned a valve, felt the air rush into my garment. As it inflated tightly against my body, I started to gasp before I remembered to adjust the oxygen supply to my helmet. Finally I turned a switch that cut me into the communication system.

"Ready?" asked Sparrow. His voice was a tinny scratch in my ears.

"Ready," grunted Big Bull. Sparrow pulled the land rover to a halt a dozen yards behind the other vehicle. I watched, sweating, as he bled the air from the cabin, opened the door and stepped outside.

Big Bull prodded me with the laser gun and I followed. Any hope of grabbing his weapon quickly was dispelled when he took a position half a dozen yards to my rear. I had to admire the technique.

The heat struck immediately. The furnace heat on my sunward side struck like a blow torch. My back, in shadow, felt numb with cold. While groping with the controls, I rotated my body slowly to help bring the temperature into balance. Sparrow and Big Bull were having similar problems.

Finally I got the controls set. If the temperature wasn't satisfactory, it at least was bearable. I returned my attention to Sparrow, who silently was regarding Mark's vehicle.

"Step outside, Randall!" His voice suddenly tinkled in my earphones. There was a long moment of silence. "Step outside before I burn you down," he rasped.

"Check the vehicle," instructed Big Bull. Sparrow started forward, his laser pointed directly at the plexidome. He attempted to peer in through the rear before sidling around to the door. Watching him, I felt I would burst with tension.

"Empty," Sparrow exclaimed jerkily. His voice, in the phones, held a touch of wonder. He grasped the handle and attempted to turn it. "It's locked from the inside."

"Impossible," said Big Bull. "Perhaps it's stuck."

"It's still empty."

"Any tracks?" Sparrow's gaze went to the crunchy surface. It was sufficiently soft that I saw the imprints of his own boots. As he moved carefully around the vehicle, I raised my eyes into the vastness beyond. A mosaic of garish light and shadow, it revealed nothing.

Sparrow completed a full circle before looking up. "They're gone . . . and no tracks." His voice was disbelieving.

"Where?" I asked apprehensively, then suddenly I knew. Mark and Ann had found their door; there could be no other answer. I wanted to shout and laugh with glee. No matter what happened, Sparrow and Big Bull had failed;

Mark and Ann were safe! It was all I could do to keep from taunting them.

"Does it matter where?" asked Sparrow. "It's a trick."

"Trick?"

"They raked their footprints clean behind them. They're hiding, desperately hoping that we'll give up and go back. Or do they sense that they're as good as dead? Tell me, Blake, do they know that?" His voice held a sadistic edge that made me grit my teeth.

"Wreck their rover," instructed Big Bull. "That'll settle the issue." Sparrow lifted the laser and pulled back on the wire looped around his index finger. A line of whitish smoke showed briefly as the beam sliced through the domed roof. A second beam destroyed the engine.

"Just like burying them both," observed Sparrow. His voice held a quiet satisfaction. He turned to look at me. "This is quite a place to die, isn't it, Blake? A man wouldn't be crowded for space." The words sent a cold chill through me.

"I wouldn't care for it," I admitted.

"But is choice an ingredient of life? Not always, Blake."

"You're trying to tell me something," I said edgily.

"Trying? No, I'm telling you."

"Kill him," interrupted Big Bull.

"Why?" I swung toward him, sick with terror.

"Why do you think?" asked Sparrow. "But you're looking the wrong way." As I twisted back, he lifted the laser.

"Wait," I cried.

"For what?" His finger came back on the wire.

Suddenly he was gone!

I stared stupidly at the spot where he'd stood. "Gone, he's gone," I shouted wildly.

"Gone," echoed Big Bull. He looked at the spot where Sparrow had stood, at the wrecked land rover, back at me. His eyes were puzzled. Abruptly his hand came up with the laser.

"Wait," I shouted, "you don't know what happened!" It was a desperate gambit to buy time, to let me grope with my thoughts.

His hand hesitated. "What happened?"

"They're gone. So has your partner."

"Any fool can see that."

"Gone into time," I cried. "They've fled into the fourth or fifth or nth dimension—perhaps into a billion years or to the other side of the universe. They'll never be back. The same thing will happen to you if you kill me."

"You're crazy."

"I am? Then what happened? You explain it."

"That's not my job."

"So what do you gain by killing me?"

"Silence, Blake. You'll never talk."

"About what?"

"I don't know." He shook his head. "I don't ask those kind of questions. They're too dangerous."

"You want to live, don't you?"

He stared at me, but suddenly I realized the stupid pig eyes weren't stupid anymore. Behind the faceplate they glowed with a faint puzzlement, an odd sort of pity. He said, "I don't want to kill you Blake. I don't like to kill." He shook his head. "Would you believe that I've never killed a man before? It isn't my nature. That's why they assigned Ryerson as my partner. He handles that department."

"Then why kill me?"

He glanced up into the black lunar sky, his eyes fixed on the crescent shape of Earth. Through his faceplate I caught a look of sadness, the sadness of a man saying farewell to his world. He looked back at the spot where Sparrow had stood before switching his eyes to me.

"Each man runs his course, Blake; each man has his job. Perhaps it's fate that we so often go unquestioning through life; I don't know. But is life as dear as all that? A man must do what he has been fashioned to do. I have no doubt that your friend was a genius, perhaps a good genius. But he didn't fit into this world, our world. The men above me understand that. I don't understand why you don't."

"He's trying to create a better world," I cried.

"Ah, but this is the world I love."

"That still doesn't explain why you have to kill me."

"Orders," he said briefly. His hand completed the movement. His finger came back on the wire and my faceplate exploded. A burning sensation ripped through my chest.

I felt myself falling, falling, falling.

TWELVE

I shuddered and moaned, fought to escape the black and starless night. Phantoms haunted my path, their banshee screams tearing like knives into my consciousness. Stars blazed, whirled, died; a whole universe died.

I was alone.

Suddenly my eyes snapped open. Looking wildly around, I realized I was lying on a cot in a small cubicle that was much like the one I'd rented in the Sinus Medii. With it came the memory of those stark moments during which Sparrow had vanished—when Big Bull's laser beam had sliced through my space helmet to sear my brain. I could all but feel my faceplate explode, see the stars reel as I fell. My God, was I crazy?

I staggered to my feet, fought to steady myself. My body was trembling and I was bathed in sweat. Sight of a small briefcase on the table told me it was my room. I looked down at my clothes; they were the same ones I'd worn to Arzachel, and on that mad flight toward Oceanus Procellarum. I groaned, wiped my face. My hand came away wet. Lord, the nightmare.

Nightmare? I jerked erect. Bert Arvid had been murdered in this same room! I could visualize the laser trench above his eyes, the terror on his face. That had been no nightmare! Burying my face in my hands I tried to think. The pursuit in the gondola! The stark moment of my death under the black lunar skies! I could still see Big Bull contemplating Earth, the sad look in his eyes before he shot me. Fighting to hold my sanity, I forced myself to go minute by minute over those last few hours.

No matter how I figured it, I was dead!

And Mark and Ann had vanished—vanished into nowhere from a stalled land rover in the midst of the most barren desert known to man. They'd found their door! The memory flooded back. But what had happened to Sparrow? He'd simply vanished; there was no other word.

I felt the panic rise within me. I was crazy, crazy, crazy. Yet I knew that I wasn't. The memories were too sharply etched. That was the damnable part. If I were crazy it would all be easy. But I was sane.

Sane and back in the room where Bert Arvid had been murdered!

"Take it easy, take it easy," I whispered. There had to be an answer. Perhaps I'd fainted, had been brought back by Big Bull. But that still didn't explain Sparrow's disappearance. Besides, I remembered the laser beam tearing through my faceplate.

I found a public phone, got the number of the local office of the Procellarum mines and put through a call. It seemed a million years before it was answered and the face of someone or other appeared on the screen. I gave my name and affiliation and asked hoarsely, "Can you give me any information about a mine worker named Mark Randall?"

"Randall?"

"Alias Fallon," I said.

"Fallon?" The name fairly exploded in my ears. "Just a moment!" The face vanished from the screen. In the silence that followed I heard the sound of frantic shouts through the receiver. A new face came on—the face of a dark, angry man with snapping black eyes.

"Who's this?" he demanded. The words all but rattled the receiver. I gave him my name, emphasizing my affiliation before I repeated my question.

"Fallon?" he thundered. "That's the fellow who stole a gondola a few hours ago—headed for Procellarum with a girl. He must have been crazy. What do you know about him?"

"Nothing," I said. "What do you know about him?"

"He's dead, I can tell you that. So's the girl."

"Dead?" I asked numbly. I swayed, tried to keep my mind from shattering.

"They abandoned the gondola out near the eastern edge of the Ocean of Storms, took off in a land rover," the other explained. "That's death."

I fought down my despair and asked, "How can you be certain?"

"That they're dead? We tracked down the land rover. It was empty, destroyed. The damn fools must have wandered off in space gear. Out there, that's death."

I clung desperately to the phone. "Was there a second land rover out there?"

"A second one? Of course not."

"No other body?" I insisted.

"Listen, are you crazy?"

"I don't know," I admitted. Wearily I hung up. That Mark and Ann had fled into the bleak wastelands of the moon was certain. That much wasn't a dream. But the second land rover wasn't there. Neither was Sparrow nor Big Bull.

Neither was my body.

When it came to that, where was Bert Arvid's body? But Bert had been right: frightening things were happening in the world. I had to smile at my own grim humor. Too numb to think, I returned to my room and fell asleep.

Fourteen hours later, when I awoke, I arranged transportation back to Earth. The freighter was old, scarred with radiation, its quarters cramped. It appeared ready for the junk heap.

I thought it the most beautiful I'd ever seen.

I'd never held a laser until the hour I returned to see Ed Carmody. But I did then; I wasn't taking a chance. Jammed in my pocket, I kept my grip firmly on it. Carmody, as far as I knew, was the only person still living who could tie me to Mark Randall. The laser was to make certain that he didn't.

The pale blonde with the pinpoint eyes looked up as I

entered the managing editor's office. "Mr. Blake," she exclaimed. "It's good to see you. How was your trip to the moon?"

"Left me breathless," I said. "Is Ed Carmody in?"

"Ed Carmody?" She looked puzzled.

"The managing editor," I said drily. "The fellow you work for."

"A joker," she replied. "If you want to see Mr. Sinclair, go right in."

"Harvey Sinclair?" I gasped.

She eyed me archly. "He is the managing editor, if you'll remember."

I gazed stupidly at her. All of a sudden I felt on the point of cracking. I asked desperately, "Have you ever heard of Ed Carmody?"

"Not that I can recall." She eyed me curiously.

"Thanks." I pulled myself together with difficulty and walked past her into the office I knew so well. Harvey Sinclair, as in past years, was sitting behind the massive desk. He appeared as plump and as jowly and as full of life as ever.

He glanced up, a quick smile on his face. "Joel, you're home! Glad to see you. Pick up anything interesting on the moon?"

"The usual." We shook hands and I plopped into a chair, taking the time to gather my thoughts. "How's Ed Carmody?" I asked.

"Ed Carmody?" He cocked his head.

"I thought you knew him."

"Can't say that I do. Who is he?"

"A news-hawk." I asked carefully, "Hear anything from Karl Burger lately?"

"Karl Burger?" Again he looked puzzled.

"The director of the BPS," I explained.

"Conrad's the director, has been for years." He eyed me quizzically over his pencil. "You all right, Joel?"

"Testing," I answered wearily. "How about Department L?"

"What's that?"

"You never heard of Department L?"

He shook his head. "All Greek, Joel. Is it something I should know about?"

"Better that you don't."

"What's this all about, Joel?"

"Just trying to straighten out my thoughts. Have you heard of Mark Randall?"

"Not since he vanished." His eyes gleamed. "Got a line on him?"

"Just wondering."

"A man of his caliber just walking away, disappearing. It seems almost impossible in this day and age." He shook his head. "Probably too much pressure. At times I feel like making the break myself. The world's getting to be a regular madhouse, Joel. I can see why you like to hit the moon occasionally. It must be quiet, peaceful."

"Very quiet."

"But it does point up one thing—how little a person, any person, is missed once he's gone. Randall was at the top of the heap, yet who gives a damn now that he's dropped from sight? A few big domes, perhaps, but that's about all."

"That's the world." I looked at him. "What do you know about Martin Wister?"

"The scientist?" Sinclair regarded me oddly. "Strange you should ask. He died last night. The story just came over the wires."

"Last night?"

"At his home in Winnetka." Sinclair nodded. "As I recall, the story gave his age as ninety-six. Was he a friend?"

"I met him once. One other question." The silence grew until I forced myself to ask, "What about Bert Arvid?"

"Did you see him on the moon?" Sinclair's interest perked up.

"I heard he was there."

Sinclair looked troubled. "He apparently suffered some kind of a nervous breakdown, went to the moon on his own. We haven't the full details yet."

"He's still on the moon?"

"In the hospital, such as it is, in the Sinus Medii. They're arranging to send him back."

"What kind of a nervous breakdown, do you know?"

"He has delusions of having been murdered. Probably too much work. We've made arrangements to send him to a clinic out west. We have every hope he'll recover."

"Did he say what happened, I mean to make him think he'd been murdered?"

"It'll take a psychiatrist to untangle that. The mind's a funny thing, Joel. At times I suspect there's a lot more to it than we know."

"A lot more," I answered.

"Well, therapy can do wonders."

"Thanks." I rose tiredly from the chair.

"Take a few days off," encouraged Sinclair. "You look tired."

"I am. Very tired."

"A bit of rest will work wonders, Joel."

At the door I turned back. "Have you ever heard of Charles Hedron?"

"Who's he?"

"A man who never was," I said. I closed the door before he could answer. The pale blonde looked coyly at me.

"Find out anything about Ed Carmody?" she asked.

"Yeah, he never existed."

"Joker," she said.

So that was it, the dead walked and the living had vanished. They were gone, just as certainly as Charles Hedron, the neo-existentialist, was gone—vanished long years before. But I remembered. If no one else did, I did.

Because I could remember from one time plane to another.

I caught the nucjet back to the Coast and drove into the hills behind the university. The house that perched like a nightbird against the sky was still deserted, still lonely. I looked at it for a long while, my memories soaring.

There was no Ed Carmody, never had been in the knowledge of Harvey Sinclair and the pale blonde with the pinpoint eyes. Neither was there a Karl Burger nor a Department L. On the surface, at least, the BPS appeared much like an ordinary policing agency—political in part, bumbling, yet somehow managing to do its job. And, as I was to learn, the BPS had no record of an agent named Sybert Ryerson, nor of one named Oscar Quinby. If Sparrow and Big Bull had ever existed, it was news to the agency.

They were gone, all gone. They had existed, but had not existed—had not because someone in another time plane had returned to readjust the past. That was the only possible explanation. The readjustments, I felt certain, had been small, and completely unnoticed except to someone who could see from one time plane to another.

That's why the dead walked.

It's why Martin Wister had lived to die peacefully in his bed, why Harvey Sinclair busied himself over his copy, why Bert Arvid was battling to save his sanity.

Why I was wandering the world again.

I'd died under a laser beam at the eastern edge of the Ocean of Storms. By all rights I should have lain there until the end of eternity. But when Mark Randall had returned to readjust the past, my murderer had been wiped from existence. Or possibly not. Possibly the lives of Sparrow and Big Bull had been redirected in childhood. If so, they might still exist. It's entirely conceivable that Karl Burger could be teaching school, that Big Bull could be road building, that Sparrow. . . .

But why go on?

I know that it was Mark Randall who had returned. He'd talked of the readjustments, of the small correction that had eliminated Charles Hedron. My God! Startled, I groped for an answer that lay just beyond the edge of my consciousness. It was there, waiting to blossom, but didn't blossom; in its place I felt a growing desperation. Mark had promised that in time I'd put the bits and pieces together. To some extent, I have.

It was because Mark did return that I'd awakened in my room in the Sinus Medii. I awoke there because I could never have left there with the agents, could never have ridden the gondola with them into the bleak wastelands of the moon, could never have pursued Mark and Ann in the land rover, could never have died under that black, star-splotched sky with the Earth hanging over me. It couldn't have happened because there'd been no agents named Sparrow and Big Bull. No Karl Burger. No Department L.

Not in this reality.

But there was more, a thought that struggled for release from deep in my mind. Mark had spoken of men making the transition throughout the ages, and doubtless it was so, for Ann had made it. But how could Mark have known about the others? How could he have known that he could return, could readjust the past? To do it he'd have to reach a certain time in the past, a certain place. How could he. . . ?

The thought burst into full consciousness, the most startling thought of all; but not the answers. Numbly I contemplated the thing which had risen in mind.

Could Mark Randall originally have come from the future? Could he, from the first, have been a technician come to readjust the past? Could all his work on Earth, his conversations with me—his surmises about the future, his planting of ideas, his flight to the moon—have been part of that readjustment?

Contemplating his incredible mind, the suspicion flowered, became all but certainty. If that were true, perhaps he hadn't been an earthling at all, but a being quite different. Perhaps he had come from the stars, perhaps from a thousand or a million or a billion years in the future! *Mark Randall, the omnipotent man! Mark ranging through time, altering the past to sculpt the perfect future*—it was entirely conceivable.

My thoughts whirled. How many times in history might he have appeared at some crucial moment to divert the human footsteps? Under what famous names might he have lived? Had this time he found a mind like his own— the mind of Ann Willett? That, too, was entirely conceivable.

The implications smash at my mind.

Joel Blake, apeman! A repeat, an echo, a shadow of the past. I, alone, know that the world around me whirls in the dawn of time. The knowledge makes me restless, the more so because I am treading a beaten path, moving through a reality that already is cosmic history. We are the laggards of our race. Because I have seen through time, my poignancy is ten thousand times worse.

Often on lonely nights I gaze at the stars, and wonder. Often I fancy I hear a voice whisper: *"We are here, Joel."* The voice brings a happiness, a sorrow, a frustration. A quiet desperation. It is then that the questions tear unrelentingly at my mind.

But the glowing stars tell me nothing.

The big shock-it-to-'em bestseller

THE PRESIDENT'S PLANE IS MISSING

by Robert J. Serling

On a calm night in a nervous world, Air Force One jets off from Andrews Air Force Base. Aboard is the President of the United States, an idolized leader whose image combines the best qualities of John Kennedy and Lyndon Johnson—but whose inner thoughts remain a dark secret even to his closest aides.

The flight is normal—until the plane is high over Arizona. Then, suddenly, before a horrified controller's eyes, the plane vanishes from the radar screen . . .

"The shock of screaming headlines—a runaway bestseller that is tense . . . frightening . . . superb."—Kansas City Star

A DELL BOOK 95c

A collection of irresistibly funny and wildly imaginative short stories by the author of **Slaughterhouse-Five** . . .

Welcome to the Monkey House

by Kurt Vonnegut, Jr.

Discover the far-out imagination and unique genius of Kurt Vonnegut, Jr. in this long-awaited volume which brings together the finest of the author's shorter works. It is a collection of funny, sad, explosive stories dealing with subjects such as sex, machines, pills, men, women, time past, present and future. The fascinating, fantastic and formidable Vonnegut magic always winds up right on target, an irresistible humor with a superb cutting edge, a storytelling talent that makes reading a pleasure as well as a mind-jolting experience. **Welcome To The Monkey House** displays the enormous range of the author's extraordinary creative vision.

Watch Out: Vonnegut is definitely habit-forming.

"Hilarious, uproarious black-logic . . . a laughing prophet of doom"   —The New York Times

"One of the best living American writers."   —Graham Greene

"George Orwell, Dr. Caligari and Flash Gordon compounded into one writer . . . In his hands the Silly Putty of contemporary aspirations becomes exploding plastic . . . a zany but moral mod scientist at the controls of a literary time machine . . . he makes his literary instrument sing."   —Time Magazine

A DELL BOOK   95c

If you cannot obtain copies of this title from your local bookseller, just send the price (plus 10c per copy for handling and postage) to Dell Books, Box 2291, Grand Central Post Office, New York, N.Y. 10017. No postage or handling charge is required on any order of five or more books.

KURT VONNEGUT, JR.

"One of the best living American writers."
—Graham Greene

Now available in paperback from Dell ...

CAT'S CRADLE
A fantasy about the end of the world—replete with atomic scientists, ugly Americans, gorgeous Sex Queens, Caribbean dictators and God.

A Dell Book: 95c
Also available as a Delta paperback: $1.65/in Canada $1.95

GOD BLESS YOU MR. ROSEWATER
A satirical and black-humored novel about Eliot Rosewater, president of the Rosewater Foundation, dedicated to bring love into the hearts of everyone.

A Dell Book: 95c
Also available as a Delta paperback: $1.75/in Canada $2.10

THE SIRENS OF TITAN
At the same time a deep and comic reflection on the human dilemma, this novel follows the richest man in America, Malachi Constant, as he gives up a life of unequaled indulgence to pursue the irresistible Sirens of Titan.

A Dell Book: 95c

WELCOME TO THE MONKEY HOUSE
The long-awaited volume which brings together the finest of Kurt Vonnegut, Jr.'s shorter works. It is a funny, sad, explosive, wildly gyrating gathering, a mind-boggling grab bag in which every selection is a winner.

A Dell Book: 95c

If you cannot obtain copies of these books from your local bookseller, just send the price (plus 10c per copy for handling and postage) to Dell Books, Box 2291, Grand Central Post Office, New York, N.Y. 10017. No postage or handling charge is required on any order of five or more books.